F E R A L
N I G H T S

CYNTHIA LEITICH SMITH

**WALKER
BOOKS**

First published 2013 by Walker Books Ltd
87 Vauxhall Walk, London SE11 5HJ

10 9 8 7 6 5 4 3 2 1

Text © 2013 Cynthia Leitich Smith
Cover photographs © 2013 Tore Thiis Fjeld / Getty Images (island);
© 2013 Morton Beebe / Corbis (cat)

This book has been typeset in Minion.

Printed and bound in Great Britain by Clays Ltd, St Ives plc

British Library Cataloguing in Publication Data:
a catalogue record for this book is available from the British Library

ISBN 978-1-4063-4328-1

www.walker.co.uk

For Anne,

who hails from a far more pleasant tropical island

"ARE YOU PREDATOR OR PREY?"

—SANGUINI'S: A VERY RARE RESTAURANT

AUSTIN, TEXAS

ninja-looking move, one I've nailed a hundred times. But not with a gun pointed at me or after slamming a six-pack of Bud Light.

Instead of landing neatly behind Grams on the plank floor, I overshoot the edge of the loft and, waving my arms for balance, fall another story down to hit the ground near the hogpen. Contrary to superstition, I don't always land on my feet.

Off-balance, I turn my ankle and, wincing, dart into the early-morning light.

I didn't feel the winter chill in the barn. Not half buried in straw with a warm, enthusiastic girl draped over me and alcohol heating my belly.

Outside, the wind bites my skin, and I yank together my unsnapped Western-style shirt. Glancing at Grams's old farmhouse, I hesitate. I don't have much in the way of belongings, but a change of clothes would be nice. Besides, it's the only home I've ever known.

Bam. Grams gets another round off. So much for that idea.

On the upside, she's a great shot. Grams must have more familial affection for me than she realizes, or I'd be dead by now. Still, it'd be idiotic to push my luck.

What the hell. It's time I moved on. Because of my grandmother, I've got no friends, and I wasn't getting much out of my senior year of high school anyway.

Within seconds, my semi-restored 1972 Mercury

11

Cougar roars to life. I make a U-turn and hit the accelerator, peeling out on the long gravel drive.

Farewell, Kansas!

I've got a few hundred bucks on my cash card. Enough to hightail it to the only family I have left — my big sister, Ruby, in Austin.

Could be the adrenaline, could be my metabolism, but I feel sober enough to drive. I stop for gas and munchies (four bacon cheeseburgers, six packs of beef jerky, and a two-liter bottle of Coke) outside Wichita, and just over an hour later, pull over in Tonkawa, Oklahoma, for a nap. I don't, strictly speaking, need the sleep, but I relish it.

Continuing on my way, I sing along to country music and the pain in my ankle fades to a dull ache. By the time I hit OK City, it's gone and the bruise has vanished, too.

Being what I am has its advantages.

I don't feel that guilty about disappointing Grams. Wind blows. Seasons change. And I hook up with nearly every smokin' girl who catches my eye. Since puberty, I've worked my way through a sizable percentage of the decent *Homo sapiens* females (and a couple of the gloriously indecent ones) near my age residing in Butler County.

So, no regrets, or at least few regrets, even if Zoë did cost me room and board.

I don't blame Grams, either. She's got a no-tolerance policy when it comes to friends, babes, or showing so much as a whisker in public — like I'd be stupid enough to tell anyone that we're werecats. I understand that it's a dangerous world, that our keys to survival are secrets, lies, and loneliness. My whole life, I've never known any different.

Cruising down I-35 South, I'm ready for something new.

CLYDE

SOMETIMES IT FEELS LIKE I'm the one haunting this little neighborhood park, but no. That's the literal domain of my best bud, Travis. The big question is why.

Why is he still here? Why isn't he resting in peace?

I start off with a safer subject, our friend Aimee. "She hasn't been to the paintball range since . . . you know," I say. We don't usually talk about the night he was murdered. "She claims nobody wants to go with her."

"Why don't you go?" Travis asks.

Maybe talking about Aimee isn't so safe after all. She's attractive enough in a friend sort of way, and her comic-book collection rivals mine. But paintball seems more like a date than just hanging out, and no way can I cross that line.

I'd never do that to Travis, especially now that he's dead.

Seated by the chain-link fence that's become a shrine to his memory, I peel a blade of dry brown grass in two. "You know I'm a lousy shot."

Partly to distract him, I display the most recent cards in a row on the paved walk, and Travis floats down for a closer look. At first, people from all over Austin—including a few ass-wipes from Waterloo High who never spoke to him when he was alive—brought not only cards ("Forever in Our Hearts") but also homemade signs ("We Love You, Travis!"), flowers, and candles. Now it's just those of us who knew him.

With the holidays came red bows, candy canes, and a beaded snowflake ornament, not that we get a lot of snow. I spot a new contribution, a four-inch-long Oaxacan wood carving of an armadillo. Like the plush dillos, it obviously was left by someone in the loose network of local shifters who knows that Travis was a werearmadillo.

"Do ghosts make New Year's resolutions?" I ask, tossing the grass aside.

"Like what?" Travis replies. "You think I should lose weight?"

"Very funny, Mr. Incorporeal." He appears vaguely

15

translucent, but otherwise looks like he always has — barrel body, bowl haircut, Longhorns jersey, and blue jeans.

Travis is the first friend I've lost . . . or sort of lost, given that his spirit is still here. As the wind picks up, blowing empty swings, it's hard to know how to feel about that.

I've been doing my homework, trying to figure out why he became a ghost in the first place. At first, I figured he was too upset to move on — pissed off at having been murdered, wanting his life back, and freaked out by the grieving of the family he left behind. But Travis doesn't seem stuck or angry. He doesn't seem lost or afraid or confused. He's not haunting his own home, where he could watch over his loved ones, and his remains were properly buried with full honors.

"Clyde," he begins, "what're you trying to get at?"

"Like . . ." I return the cards to the fence, use the links to raise myself, and maneuver into my wheelchair. "Maybe you should think about, you know, going into the Light."

Travis's grin is good-natured. "What would you do without me?"

"I'm just saying," I reply. "It's been a while since . . . it happened." Travis was slaughtered near this very spot — closer to the tennis courts — over three months ago by a skanky werecat named Ruby Kitahara, who hasn't been seen or heard from since.

When he doesn't reply, I add, "Do you want to talk about it?"

It has to be painful, discussing your own murder. Travis didn't even reveal his ghostly self to me until the twenty-first of December (I swallowed my gum), and other than during one disastrous road trip, I'd been coming here at least twice a week since he died back in September.

"I've told you," Travis replies. "It was Friday the thirteenth. Ruby said she needed to talk. She invited me out for a walk in the park, and so I went."

I zip my jacket. My wereopossum metabolism usually keeps me warm enough, but Travis's spiritual presence has a chilling effect. Like a ghostly mini air conditioner.

Resisting the temptation to come right out and call him a dumbass, I say, "A badly lit, secluded park on Friday the thirteenth, and you knew she was a werepredator, and you went anyway?"

He hangs his head, hunches his shoulders, and suddenly I feel lousy for picking on the dead guy. "Yeah."

I wave my hand dismissively. "I know. Ruby is hot, hotty, hotness personified — evil of course, but abso-freaking-lutely four-alarm, red smokin' hot." I may have overstated my point. "I would've gone, too."

You have to watch out for Cat people. They use sex like a weapon.

"Ruby was saying something about the local cops when she suddenly froze and her claws came out. She hissed at me to beat it, and I did. I hauled butt."

It goes without saying that Dillos aren't particularly speedy.

"When I looked back," Travis concludes, "she'd forced a quick shift — it had to have hurt — and then sprang off in animal form. I'd just made it to the parking lot when paws slammed me to the ground." He shudders. "The last thing I remember is saber teeth sliding into the back of my neck." Travis rubs the area as if it still hurts.

Despite werecats' typical BS about their being distantly related to sabertooth tigers (or at least sabertooth were-tigers), no known modern species of Cat have teeth that extend past their jaws. However, they insist on referring to their canines as "saber teeth" because the word *canine* has such a strong Coyote/Wolf connotation.

"Ruby lured you out and let you have a head start so she could chase you," I realize out loud. "I guess it's true what they say. Cats love to play with their food."

"Why me?" Travis asks. "I wasn't a fast runner. If she was looking for sport . . ."

"She's a Cat," I remind him. "They think with their stomachs and genitals. Logic doesn't apply." Shifter-on-shifter violent crime is rare, though, except between certain longtime warring groups like Lions and Hyenas or Orcas and Seals.

"Has there been any progress with the police investigation?" he wants to know.

I've hounded Detectives Zaleski and Wertheimer for details, but they've as much as admitted that the case is getting colder every day. They insist they're not giving up, and I guess it's possible there's stuff they're not telling me.

After all, I'm not only a sixteen-year-old civilian. I'm also a poster child for everyone who's ever gotten their booty kicked. My parents, my friends, the cops — everyone's overprotective of me.

Realizing Travis is still waiting for an answer, I say, "They're trying, but —"

"I know," he replies. "They've got a lot of other things to worry about." And it's not like any case, even a murder, is as important to them as this one is to us.

Travis dematerializes without saying good-bye, and who can blame him? My own best friend was mauled to death, partly eaten, and what have I done about it?

Come to think about it, *that* must be why my Dillo pal is haunting this park — the scene of the crime — and why I'm the only one he's shown himself to.

Travis's killer — Ruby Kitahara — is living free and easy and without regrets. If he's to have any hope of resting in peace, he needs me to find her.

He needs me to make her pay for what she's done.

The babies are screaming. Clara is screaming in the nursery down the hall. Claudette is screaming in the kitchen

19

sink. Cleatus is screaming in the bouncer chair in front of the TV, and Clint is screaming in the playpen while pointing at Scooby on-screen.

"Clyde," Dad calls, "do something!" He's supposedly bathing Claudette.

If the kits were quints instead of quads, I might be a reality-TV star by now, bitching about the paparazzi, accompanied by nubile twenty-something personal assistants/au pairs, but alas, a grand total of five kids doesn't cut it.

Still, if more humans were shifter-friendly, the Possum angle might've sold the show. I could've launched an improv career with off-color jokes about my prehensile tail.

"Pick one!" my father yells. "Cleatus! He's closest."

Cleatus just took a dump, and it's his squalling that set off the others.

Holding my breath, I maneuver the chair to scoop up the stinky baby in one arm and roll down the hall to the changing table in the nursery.

It isn't usually only Dad and me versus the bellowing horde, but Mom ducked out to pick up diapers fifteen minutes ago, which is apparently two minutes longer than we can handle the kits without the house falling into chaos. It's not our fault. Possum babies are biologically hardwired to cling to their mothers.

It takes some doing to get Cleatus wiped, powdered, and relocated to his crib, but fortunately, my parents found a wheelchair-accessible changing table. Then I roll across the room to cheer up Clara by shaking a rattle and making monkey noises.

Back in the family room, Clint's wailing comes to a hiccupping halt as my soaking-wet dad slips a freshly towel-dried Claudette into the bouncer chair. "Let's wait until your mother comes home to bathe the rest."

Multiple births are over fifty percent more common among werepeople than humans. But Dad spent much of the past several years working at an oil rig in the Gulf, so I was an only child until the kits were born.

I love the little poopers, and I like having my father around again.

It's hard on a family, being apart.

My parents even separated for a while, but after I was born, they fell back into a rhythm together. When the quads came, Dad had to commit more face time to the family. Now he's studying to get certified as a science teacher and overparenting me out of guilt because he wasn't around much when I was growing up.

Turning down the TV, he says, "I've been meaning to have a talk with you."

"Again?" At his expression, I add, "I aced Driver's Ed. I know how to tie a tie, and I learned everything I need to know about sex from the Internet."

He plops into the sofa chair. "About that monstrosity of an SUV . . ."

The car was a gift from my friend Quincie, who sort of

inherited it. Other than this afternoon's child-care break, Dad and I have spent the day sprucing it up. I can't wait to show Aimee. "I can afford the gas. Or at least I'll be able to once I get that raise —"

"I'd feel better about your working if your grades were better." Dad stands and navigates around the toys on the floor to the Christmas tree. "But it's more than that." He unravels a strand of popcorn from the branches. "You've had a lot to deal with lately — the babies, your physical therapy, my moving back in, and what happened to Travis."

Dad missed the funeral. Up to this point, only Mom has brought up Travis's death. I can't tell them about my newfound mission to find his killer. They worry enough as it is.

"You're in a growth spurt, too," Dad adds. "You're tall for a Possum, filling out."

"Hadn't noticed," I reply, though I did get new clothes for solstice and Christmas. Stuck in this chair, constantly looking up at other people, it's hard to feel tall.

"I bet Aimee has noticed," Dad says.

Now we're getting down to it. Nice man, my father. Not known for his subtlety.

"We're just friends," I reply, plucking a sticky discarded pacifier from between the couch cushions. I set it on the coffee table to be washed. "You don't like Aimee?"

She isn't one of us, so to speak. My father has always seemed open-minded about others — humans

22

and non-Possum shifters. But parents tend be more conservative when romance (and/or the possibility of sex) is involved, and Mom and Dad were "taken aback," as they put it, by the matching half-inch-tall crosses that Aimee and I had inked around our necks.

"Aimee was Travis's girl," I explain. "I'm keeping an eye on her for him. You know, to honor his memory." It's a phrase I picked up at the funeral.

Dad drops the string of popcorn into a trash bag. "I didn't realize."

I shrug. "Now you do."

AIMEE

"THE KEY TO GRADUATING from sidekick to hero," Clyde says, "is all about the car."

"The car?" I can barely hear him above the din of the bustling restaurant kitchen where we work part-time as dishwashers. By "we," I mostly mean "me."

As usual, he's busier running his mouth than the sprayer. That's okay. As much as I love this place, our particular jobs aren't super interesting. "What about the car?" I ask.

Clyde recently procured an ugly beige SUV, a major trade-up from his old compact, and he's been obsessing over it ever since.

"Think about it," he replies, scraping plates clean. "Does Robin drive the Batmobile? Does Wonder Girl fly the invisible plane?"

"They have the power to fly independently," I point out. "So why do the Wonders even need a plane?"

"Way back, she — never mind. That's not the point. There *is* an invisible plane, and Wonder Girl *never* flies it."

"Which Wonder Girl?" I counter. "Donna Troy or Cassie —?"

"Doesn't matter," he says, clearly impatient. "Neither of them flies the plane."

"Are you sure?" Arguing with Clyde is usually an ordeal, but I enjoy it. "What about Drusilla, from the old *Wonder Woman* TV show?" We rented and watched it over the holidays. The World War II episodes are more fun than the "modern-era" ones.

"She's not canon!" Clyde exclaims.

I don't bring up the more recent animated productions. We have a pact to always discuss those separately.

It's ten minutes after six. Sanguini's is always booked solid, but Saturdays are especially intense. Using my sleeve, I wipe my forehead. The restaurant just opened at sunset, but we had prep dishes to take care of first.

"Hey, kids!" The manager, Sergio, offers us each a glass. "Take ten."

I immediately chug my ice water as a couple of the waiters snag their appetizer orders. One is decked out in a red satin shirt and black leather pants, complete with a high-necked cape. The other is costumed as a Turok-Han vamp.

That's not unusual around here. The shtick is that this Italian restaurant is supposedly staffed by the undead. Consequently, dining-room employees model Goth-style attire, and the majority of guests arrive similarly or at least spookily dressed. It's paranormal cosplay to the nth degree. Pretend, most of the time.

"Here, take these!" Sergio presents Clyde and me with personalized business cards, both with the title *Culinary Engineer*. "Every Sanguini's employee is an essential team member," he insists. "We all contribute to making this place a success. Let me know tonight if you want any changes, and you can pick up a box of them with your check next Friday."

It's my first business card. Nifty. I thank Sergio, slip it in my wallet, and head out to take ten with Clyde. We exit the building via the rear ramp, and he rolls to the parking lot. He's doing better with the wheelchair, and pushing it has built up his arms.

Last fall, Clyde was critically injured in a real-life vampire attack. It took powerful healing magic to pull him out of the subsequent coma. Despite physical therapy and his heightened wereopossum healing abilities, he's still on the mend.

I double-take at the vehicle in the handicapped spot. "Is *that* your car?"

Under the overhead light, the once-beige Ford Explorer is covered with gleaming dominoes — from roof to hubcaps, everything but the windows, mirrors, tires, and license plate . . . hundreds, maybe thousands of them.

When I glance down for an answer, Clyde isn't in his wheelchair. He takes a few halting steps on the asphalt — the first time I've seen him stand on his own since being injured. "These dominoes were made from shifter bones."

"Bones?" I move in for a closer look, determined not to make too big of a deal out of the fact that he's walking. Clyde gets self-conscious easily.

"Some people collect them," he informs me.

"Isn't that sacrilegious?" I hesitate. "Or at least disrespectful?"

Clyde bristles. "Collecting them or my sticking them on my car?"

I was thinking both, actually, but I let it go. As a human being, it's really not my place to lecture him on what shape-shifters should find offensive.

In the past year, my social circle expanded to include the furry, feathered, and armored after I became close friends with a sweetheart of a werearmadillo named Travis through the Environmental Club at school. He was considerate and gentlemanly (and okay, kind of lumpy-looking). When it comes to guys, I prefer substance over style.

Travis was my "almost" first love, my "maybe" first

love. Then last September someone tore him into bloody pieces before we could figure "us" out.

A customer in skull makeup and a black leather jacket parks his motorcycle in the next row as Clyde announces, "I've decided to call the car 'the Bone Chiller,' because it's covered in bones, the sight of it will chill evildoers, and it's so cool, it's chilly."

Uh-huh. Truth is, I find his dorkiness endearing. After all, I know as much about superhero sidekicks as he does. Waiting for the guy decked out as Ghost Rider to boogie on by, I try to pull a domino off the hood and can't. "How did you —?"

"My dad helped me. It took most of the day." Clyde's on a roll. "I was researching ghosts over the holidays — spirits usually hang around because of unfinished business or because their remains weren't properly put to rest — and I came across these dominoes on eBay. I bid on a crate for fifty bucks and won."

Okay. "But why —?"

"The last time we faced down the supernatural, it royally kicked our ass." Clyde runs a hand through his very prematurely gray-speckled dark hair. "I'd rather not be caught flat again. Anyway, there's no way of reuniting these bones with their original owners, so I'm making a statement. I'm taking them back on behalf of shifters everywhere. I'm giving them a chance to reclaim their dignity."

Reclaim their dignity? Did he just say that out loud? Having been seriously injured has changed Clyde. He's deeper than he used to be. He cares more.

"It's not bad enough that werepeople are fair game to humans and the undead," Clyde adds. "We even target each other."

"Werepeople" is the preferred term for shape-shifters, but it's controversial. The prefix "were" actually means "man." So, by calling themselves werepeople, shifters are denying their animal form, which is a huge part of their identity.

I shush him as a couple dressed as a voodoo priestess and witch doctor get out of a Volvo with California license plates. Once they're on their way, Clyde announces, "It has to stop. We can't go on killing each other, the way Ruby Kitahara killed Travis. I'm going to make an example out of her. I'm going to make sure she's punished for what she's done."

Oh. Well. Clyde's channeling his inner superhero all right, but neither of us is the muscle of our little social circle. Quincie P. Morris, who inherited Sanguini's from her late parents, is a wholly souled vampire (the cuddly, nonhomicidal kind). Her boyfriend, Kieren Morales, is a werewolf, and Zachary is the "slipped" (not fallen) guardian angel assigned to watch over her. They all just left town together to visit some friend of Zachary's in

Vermont. Clyde and I weren't invited — not that, after the Michigan fiasco, our parents probably would've let us go along anyway.

Trying to track a murderous werecat like Ruby without our big guns . . . "Clyde, think about what you've been through. Do you honestly —?"

"You don't think I can cut it?" He crosses his hairy arms over his thin chest. "I don't strike you as a man of action? I'll have you know —"

"I don't want anything terrible to happen to you!" I yell. "You know, again." I take a breath. "It wasn't that long ago that you almost died."

"Oh, right," Clyde replies because, shifter or not, he sucks at dealing with emotions as much as most teenage boys.

As much as my head hates his Super Possum idea, my heart finds it romantic. Except I see myself by his side. I imagine us being like Oliver Queen/Green Arrow and Dinah Lance/Black Canary.

No, forget that. I'm not that big on fishnets, and talk about relationship issues!

More like Barbara Gordon/Batgirl/Oracle and Dick Grayson/Robin/Nightwing — two sidekicks who grow into their legends as their friendship blossoms to more. . . .

Granted, they have their issues, too.

Love is scary hard, even for superheroes.

Not that it matters, because we are talking *Clyde* after

all, and I could whack him over the head with a brick and he wouldn't notice I'm a girl.

Ignoring the gang of "Thriller"-esque zombies that just lurched out of a minivan, I offer a hand to help him back into the wheelchair. "I can't talk you out of this?"

"No way," he says.

"Then count me in," I reply. "But for the record, I'm not your sidekick."

YOSHI

WHAT GRAMS NEVER UNDERSTOOD is that I don't just fool around with girls.

I appreciate them. All shapes. All sizes. All humanoid species. I adore them, and not just for their "feminine wiles," as she likes to say.

True, Mom abandoned me as a cub, and I never knew my father. But I've always had my sister, Ruby. For that matter, until now, I've always had Grams herself. I may not like the old puss, but, especially now that she's of my past, I kind of miss her.

When I want an actual conversation, I go to Ruby. Or at least I did until she left home. My sister hugged me good-bye over a year ago. It was after winter finals of her first semester at Butler Community College. She told Grams that she'd applied on the Internet and landed a six-month internship in music promotion in Austin. She'd be working with some guy named Paxton.

"He's a Cat, too," she informed me.

Discussing one's species with a stranger online struck me as a stupid idea. Groups like the National Council for Preserving Humanity troll the Web for shifters to target. And then there are the opportunists. Our animal-form bodies are stuffed and displayed in natural history museums. Our animal-form pelts are sold by black-market furriers, and our bones are ground and marketed as aphrodisiacs.

But my sister was fine. For months, she was fine. She sounded happy even.

Ruby never came home, but she called, e-mailed, and texted.

Then, without warning, Grams and I didn't hear from her again. Not after last September. Not even two weeks ago, on my eighteenth birthday.

I've been worried, I admit it. But now that I'm on my own for the first time, I can appreciate how amazing it is. So Ruby got busy, lost track of time. Maybe even fell in love. So what? She'll be jazzed to see me.

This is my first trip outside the Midwest, and I cannot get over the weather. It's almost sixty degrees. In January.

Passing an outdoor vendor hawking tie-dyed clothing, I spot honest-to-God palm trees and a skinny man dressed in only a thong riding a bike.

"It's around here somewhere," I mutter to myself, searching for Ruby's place on South Lamar. I pull into a strip-mall parking lot and scan the storefronts. An art-supply store. A yoga studio. A place that sells musical instruments.

Home Post Office matches the address I have for my sister.

I'd been hoping to find Ruby herself, or at least her apartment.

Lacking any better ideas, I go inside the mail store, triggering a small bell above the glass door. The clerk is young, thin, and lanky. He has acne and huge, blond, frizzy hair. The name tag on his white polo shirt reads *Timothy*. He smells like weed.

"Can I help you?" he asks, glancing up from a Victoria's Secret catalog.

"I'm looking for someone who rents a box here," I begin. "Ruby or Rubina—"

"Rubina?" He straightens behind the counter. "Sorry, man, I'm not allowed to give out any information—"

"But you do know her?" I say. "Long black hair, slender, *hapa*—you know, half white, half Japanese?" Being her kid brother doesn't blind me to the fact that Ruby's unforgettable. "Look, she's my sister, and—"

"I see the family resemblance," he replies. "You're taller, though."

You think? "This is the only address I have, and she never checks messages."

Timothy keys in her name, finds the number, then picks up a phone to call. Seconds later, he says, "This is Timothy at Home Post Office. Your brother stopped by, looking for you." He leaves a number and hangs up. "She never checks messages?"

"Free spirit," I explain.

Timothy laughs. "Yeah, me too, but I live for my phone. She didn't give a street address, but . . ." He ducks behind a half wall to an intake-distribution room lined with lockboxes.

A moment later, Timothy comes back and spreads out two business cards and a slightly stained, torn piece of ruled paper on the counter. "You're not the only one looking for her. These people all asked me to call if she shows again."

If? "How long has it been since she picked up her mail?"

He frowns as if thinking it over. "A few months."

Months? The first card is printed with the name Karl Richards of Richards Heating & Air-Conditioning. The little logo in the corner depicts a turquoise-blue armadillo, wearing a scarf. The second is from Detective Konstantine Zaleski of the Austin Police Department. And on the scrap paper, someone has hand-scrawled *Clyde* and a phone

35

number. Before Timothy can protest, I swipe up all three. "Thanks."

"Want to leave your digits?" he asks. "In case she calls back?"

I scribble them down and turn to leave.

Finally, Timothy sees fit to inform me: "I know where she works."

My smile is forced. "You don't say?"

"Sanguini's," he declares like that's supposed to mean something. "Ruby is — or at least used to be — their spokesmodel or whatever."

Spokesmodel? Ruby's notoriously camera shy. She didn't mention a new job, and she's not the type who enjoys being the center of attention. "What kind of place is it?"

"A restaurant." Timothy rattles off directions.

YOSHI

THE OLD ONE-STORY brick building doesn't look like much on the outside. As I pass through the parking lot, the most remarkable thing is that it doesn't have any windows.

I don't like that. It suggests a trap.

The Saturday night crowd doesn't seem worried. They radiate Goth to giddy; sassy spookiness to S&M. A trio dressed as fairies (sparkly violet wings) skips by, holding hands and giggling. A woman in a raspberry-colored minidress slinks out of a shiny black Mercedes-Benz, carrying a crop. She's joined by a devil in a black suit with a red satin cape and convincing horns.

Coming around the building, a vixen with a Cheshire grin holds open the front door for me. She exudes feline

37

in her laced-up, push-up, low-cut, tiger-striped, skintight custom bodysuit.

I appreciate any girl in a catsuit, even if it is false advertising.

Inside the restaurant foyer, the decadent aromas are almost overwhelming. I make out the scents of roasting garlic, rattlesnake, alligator, boar. . . .

Once the diners ahead of me are seated, I approach the desk.

"Welcome to Sanguini's." As the hostess glances up from her leather-bound reservation book, I notice the embroidered black flowers barely covering her more enticing bits beneath the otherwise sheer black dress.

"Are you predator or prey?" she asks.

"Hmm?" I blink back up at her face. "Oh, right. I'm here to see my sister, Ruby."

"Davidson Morris's . . . friend Ruby?" she asks with finely arched brows.

Never heard of him, but Ruby's not a common name. "Possibly."

"I'm sorry. Ruby Kitahara is no longer with the restaurant" is the answer.

When I just stand there, blank, she adds, "Let me find a manager to help you."

A guy with a Celtic-style cross carved into his 'fro guides me through heavy long red drapes and into the dining room. Though the building is old, the interior has been newly remodeled. I register the gleaming crystal chandelier, the deep-blue carpeting, and the crimson napkins folded into the shape of bats.

A passing waiter in a black sequined sheath has shellacked his silvery hair to fan out six inches around his face. Two buxom women — I assumed they're wearing clothes, but it looks like lavender body paint — lean over deviled eggs to kiss, and I catch a flash of tongue. From hidden speakers, Frank Sinatra sings "Days of Wine and Roses."

"This way," my escort says, and I realize I've paused to drool.

The guy abandons me in the manager's office, saying someone will be right there, and shuts the door behind him. It's a bland, fairly utilitarian space. A desk. Two chairs. A filing cabinet and a tropical tree — make that a fake tropical tree.

I pace the tight perimeter once. Twice. Check my watch. Sit.

Two minutes later, a teenager staggers in. In his damp white T-shirt and jeans, he doesn't look like he belongs at the restaurant. Taking jerky, pained steps, he touches the brick wall for support before settling behind the desk and introduces himself as Clyde.

Is this the Clyde who left his number with Timothy at Home Post Office?

My nose identifies him as a wereopossum. He's no doubt recognized me (and possibly Ruby before me) as a Cat the same way.

"So you're Ruby Kitahara's brother." He taps his finger-claws, slightly extended, against the desktop. "And you don't know where she is, either?"

"Just hit town," I explain, "and I can't seem to get ahold of her." It's none of his business, but I'm trying to play nice. "She hasn't called home lately."

Clyde takes that in. "And home is?"

"Kansas," I reply. "Is a manager still on the way?"

"Yes." He steeples his fingertips. "What's your name?"

"Yoshi." The kid has tiny crosses tattooed around his neck. "Yoshi Kitahara." He's probably intimidated because I'm a werepredator, and he's a goofy-looking animal form. I try small talk. "What do you do around here, bus tables?"

He narrows his dark eyes. "Yoshi, nobody has seen your sister since mid-September. She was involved with Davidson Morris, who was the manager at the time."

" 'Involved with' as in 'dating'?" I ask. "I don't think so."

Something isn't right. The manager should've showed by now. I want out of this cramped room. Standing, I reach for the filing-cabinet drawer labeled "Employee Records."

"Hey!" Clyde exclaims. "Those are private."

Not for long. Old-fashioned, using paper, but more

convenient for me. I yank the drawer open, breaking the lock. "All I want is my sister's home address."

"Ruby never had an official file," Clyde informs me. Using the desk for leverage, he rises from the chair. "You're sure you don't know where she is?"

I check to confirm he's right, that there's no file, and lean against the cabinet. "What's she to you?"

He bares tiny, pointed teeth. "Ruby killed one of my best friends."

It's such a melodramatic thing to say, I can't help laughing. "That's ridiculous."

The Possum raises his chin — to me, a *Puma concolor sapiens*. He's deadly serious, fiercely intense. No wonder he's already going gray.

"His name was Travis," the boy declares. "He was a Dillo, only sixteen years —"

"Sorry about your loss," I counter. "But you've got the wrong Cat."

Ruby may be a predator by birth, but she's also squeamish. When she was eight, my sister went on a hunger strike until Grams promised never to roast any of our own animals again. Ruby named every last chick on the farm and made a pet of her prize hog, Wilbur. No way would she take a life, certainly not a fellow shifter's.

"She wasted two cops, too," Clyde adds. "Or at least she killed one and was an accessory to the murder of the other."

41

Like he even knows what "accessory" means. "I'm out of here."

He steps to the side, wobbling. "You're not going anywhere. Two werebears are guarding that door until Detective Zaleski gets here."

Now he's *threatening* me? It has to be a bluff, but I recognize the cop's name from one of the business cards I picked up at the mail store.

Calling my inner Cat, I welcome the ripple of fur across my face, the return of my saber teeth and claws. "You do realize, Clyde, that this means we're trapped in here together?"

He hollers, "Olek! Uri!"

I let my mouth drop open and inhale. I don't smell any Bears.

Swinging the office door open, I'm suddenly faced with a total cutie pie in a wet white apron. She has a small silver hoop threaded through her left eyebrow and, like Clyde, a ring of cross tats around her neck. Her shoulder-length blond curls are striped a moss green, and she has the most adorable cleft in her nose.

If I had to guess, I'd say she's an elfin line cook. But her ears aren't pointed, and her scent is that of a marinara-tinged human being. I hear her gulp, the rise in her heartbeat. Most girls would be afraid. She's enticed.

From behind me, Clyde shouts, "Aimee, where's security?"

"Stuck behind a fender bender on Mopac Expressway," she replies, blinking at my Cat-man face as if I were Adonis with whiskers.

It's then that I believe the werebears actually exist. That they might show up any minute and hold me for some Texas cop who suspects my sister of multiple murders.

Retracting my shift, I brush past the girl — Aimee — and hurry down the hall to the back exit. Coming around a domino-covered SUV, I weave between parked vehicles and past an athletic-looking Buffy wannabe with long blond hair in a dark trench coat, carrying a stake.

Seconds later, as I hit my ignition, I hear Aimee calling my name.

Too late. I have such a big head start that I might as well be gone already.

I spare one more glance at her, standing in the back doorway of the restaurant. She's really something. The kind of girl you've known your whole life — gone fishing with, joked with over algebra or while detasseling corn — and then one day you look up and realize she's quietly exquisite. Except that I just saw her for the first time, and she already has that effect on me. Not that it matters, because I'll never see her again and she's apparently friends with that delusional idiot Possum.

As I turn onto Congress Avenue, my cell buzzes.

"This is Karl Richards," a man says, "of Richards Heating & Air-Conditioning." He informs me that Timothy from

43

Home Post Office called him to say I swung by and invites me to compare notes on my sister's whereabouts.

The connection is sketchy. I can't make out every fourth word.

"Meet me at this address," Richards concludes, rattling it off. "It's a warehouse. Say, half an hour?" He ends the call.

I slow to a stop at Live Oak Street. Ruby is missing, apparently suspected of murder. Perfect strangers want to chase me with werebears, turn me in to the local cops, and lure me to remote buildings.

This country boy's no idiot. It's past time I figured out what's going on.

CLYDE

AT SANGUINI'S BACK EXIT, Aimee says, "We lost him."

I should've never left the chair behind. I would've been faster on wheels. "We'll call the Dillos, Zaleski, patrol the neighborhood. If Yoshi's looking for Ruby, he won't stray far. She was last seen on Academy —"

Just then Sergio bursts through the crimson drapes into the hall. He checks the manager's office, sees that it's empty, and begins, "What happened to —?"

"He got away," I explain. "Aimee and I are going after —"

"No," Sergio says. "Whatever it is, no, you're not. At least not right now."

I gape. "But —"

He pats my shoulder. "You have jobs to do here."

Sergio tightens his ponytail and heads into the kitchen. I'm not sure how much he knows about Travis's murder and Ruby's part in it. But Sergio's a smart guy, a "people" person, and humans have instincts, too.

"Can you cover for me at the sink?" I ask.

"One sec." Aimee ducks into the office and returns with a pen. "Yoshi has Kansas license plates," she informs me, writing the number on my hand.

"You memorized his license plate?" I exclaim. I didn't even think of that.

"I'm not a car person, but it's a long body style from the sixties or seventies," she goes on. "Turquoise. The paint looks new. Coming out of the lot, he turned south at the alley."

"Got it," I say. "This will help a lot." I grin. "Aimee, I could just kiss you."

"Really?" she replies, preening. "What are you waiting for?"

I wish she wouldn't joke around like that, but I guess I started it. "Tell Sergio I'll just be a minute." Gesturing toward the john, I add, "I'm going to call Zaleski."

On her way through the swinging kitchen door, Aimee warns, "Three minutes."

Detective Zaleski is a werebear, somehow related to the

restaurant's MIA bouncers. They're his nephews or cousins or something.

Given that human cops don't tend to pursue shifter-on-shifter crimes, he and his partner make such cases an unofficial priority. They're our system within the system.

I wait until the guy in the ass-less black leather pants washes up and leaves, double-check to make sure the stalls are empty, and make the call.

Once I've filled him in, Zaleski asks, "How about the kid himself? Height? Weight? Coloring?"

I close my eyes, conjuring up a mental picture. "Not quite six foot. He's in good shape — like he's worked construction . . . or on a farm. You can tell he's Ruby's brother, but his eyes are brown, not green. Oh, and he has a serious affection for product."

"Product?" the detective asked.

"Hair gel," I clarified. "He's one smug, country-fried SOB. He has on a blue Western shirt and faded jeans, torn at the knee. In shift, his fur darkens to almost black."

"You saw him in Cat form?" Zaleski exclaims. "In the restaurant?"

"Only partly, and not in a public area," I reply. "Face, teeth, and claws. He retracted it before anyone except Aimee and I got a good look at him."

The detective beeps off without saying thank you, but

I know he's grateful to finally have something solid to gnaw on.

Werepeople avoid hospitals. Our birth certificates and immunization records are always faked. So we're intentionally a lot harder to track than humans. Plus Ruby never mentioned any family or being from Kansas. Actually, she didn't so much talk to people as hang all over Davidson Morris and make catty or flirty or purring noises.

I rejoin Aimee, tackling the dishes. Avoiding any mention of species or murder, I update her on what happened between me and Yoshi in the manager's office. "He's all we've got," I conclude, scraping leftover *linguini l'autumno* into the trash can. "Not that we still *have* him, but he might know something that'll lead us to Ruby."

"And if we do find her?" Aimee asks, wielding the sprayer. "What then?"

I get her meaning. Hand-to-hand, paw-to-claw, the two of us couldn't hold Ruby long enough for help to arrive. "I'm working on it," I reply. "When the time comes, I'll know what to do." It sounds lame, even to me.

Aimee opens the steaming, stainless-steel dishwasher, pulls out a rack of newly cleaned wineglasses, and reaches for the polishing cloth. "You know, it's been almost four months since Ruby disappeared. If we haven't seen her, the cops haven't been able to find her, and her brother is looking, too, it's possible —"

"She's dead." I grit my teeth. "It'd be nice to know that for sure."

Aimee begins hand-drying the glassware. "You know how I feel about what happened to Travis," she says. "I meant it when I said I'd help you, but this whole mission thing suddenly feels more —"

"Real?" I ask as a busser drops off more dishes.

"Dangerous," Aimee replies.

YOSHI

WISHING MY CAR wasn't so conspicuous, I circle west and point it north on Lamar Boulevard. Minutes later, I spot a high-end grocery store where I grab a cup of hot tea and a slab of barbecue ribs from the dining-on-the-run aisle. I take the meal outside and choose one of the empty tables on the deck overlooking a playscape. The locals may think it's too cold tonight, but I appreciate the opportunity to sit alone under the stars.

The meat smells like heaven, though the sauce tastes a tad too sweet. I'm biased against any barbecue not from Kansas City, but the Texans don't do a half-bad job.

Pausing to wipe my fingers, I use my phone to key in a Web search and pull up dozens of articles about Sanguini's. The original chef was murdered last August.

Weeks later, the manager at the time, Davidson Morris, along with the replacement chef, Bradley Sanguini, and a local high-school vice principal were named prime suspects. Morris and the VP were found dead before they could be arrested. No word on "Sanguini," which was supposedly only a stage name.

Earlier this evening, the hostess asked me if I was looking for Davidson Morris's Ruby. Is it his fault that my sister is missing, in trouble?

I recognize her in the online photos, but it's like she's dolled up for Halloween. Ruby has added a bold white streak to her hair and gone heavy on the makeup. The black eyeliner and lipstick aren't half as attention-getting, though, as the outfits.

I don't need to see that much of my sister's cleavage. Nobody does.

At the *whoosh* of the opening store doors, I glance at three blondes in sorority T-shirts, carrying trays of salads and coffee. Normally, I'd mosey on over and make plans to meet up with at least one of them later. Not tonight.

I return my attention to the screen. Karl Richards's name pulls up a handful of links related to his heating-and-air-conditioning business, a couple about the Greater Austin Chamber of Commerce, and one fairly recent obituary.

51

I click the latter and start reading.

It notes that Travis Reid, age sixteen, was "called home by our Heavenly Father on September 13. Reid was a sophomore at Waterloo High School, where he belonged to the Environmental Club and the Spanish Club. He was preceded in death by his grandmother Christina Acosta. Survivors include his parents, Isabel and David Reid; his sister, Sierra; his grandparents Barbara and Clarence 'Dutch' Reid; his grandfather Karl Richards. . . ."

Oh, hell. Karl Richards is the grandfather of the dead teenage werearmadillo.

A car door shuts. A stout, middle-aged man in a badly fitting suit is purposefully headed my way. I make a show of yawning and stand, leaving my trash on the table.

I stroll toward the grocery-store doors and, out of the corner of my eye, notice him picking up the pace. So I veer right and turn around the back of the building.

Once I'm out of his sight, I quickly check to make sure no one's watching and then spring up the side of the wall. Latching on to the shingled roof with extended claws, I swing one leg over, then the other. I slip off my shoes, stay low, and cross the roof.

From below, my pursuer lets out a frustrated grunt. I've lost him.

I need to stay lost. My car is parked in the front lot, and I won't leave it. Better to get gone fast. But it would be stupidly showy to leap down in front of the busy market.

Fortunately, the dark of night and a row of ferns hanging above the shopping carts provide enough cover for me to slip down unnoticed, at least in theory.

A guy carrying a jug of organic detergent glances from me up to the roof.

"Excellent view," I explain. "Have a nice night."

On the lookout for my pursuer, I hurry past the spaces reserved for the disabled customers and those with small children. I'm parked another two spots down, between a Harley-Davidson motorcycle and a Smart Car.

Still carrying my running shoes, I reach for my door handle.

Then a rumbling voice says, "Yoshi Kitahara?"

It's the biggest, broadest man I've ever seen. His suit is wrinkled. His tie is loose. Werebear, I'd bet on it. I ask, "Do I know you?"

"Detective Zaleski of the Austin Police Department," he replies. "The gentleman you so gracefully ditched over there is my partner, Wertheimer." He thinks it's funny.

I default to charm. "Officer, I'm confused. I didn't do anything —"

"Did someone named Karl Richards contact you?" he asks, scratching his beard.

I can't think of a reason not to admit it. "He called and asked me to meet him."

"Don't. The werearmadillos think your sister murdered their young prince. They're out for blood."

CLYDE

IN THE BREAK ROOM, Aimee uses her fork to swirl cognac-cream fettuccine Alfredo with broiled alligator while I pick live crickets out of a squat glass jar. Nora, the chef, keeps a stock on hand for me to snack on. It's a Possum thing. "About Yoshi—"

"You're obsessing." Aimee dabs her lips with a napkin. "I only saw him for a few seconds, but . . . Well, I've seen a wereperson transform before. Or at least start to."

I've never exhibited so much as a hint of my bald tail to Aimee.

"When Yoshi retracted his shift, it was different," she adds. "He didn't seem like he was in pain or that it was a strain on his body. I didn't hear any bones grind or pop.

It was seamless, like magic or time-lapse photography. The fur practically melted away as he morphed back to fully human form."

I drop a squirming cricket into my mouth and crunch. "Anything else?"

Her expression turns dreamy. "His human face is as remarkable as his Cat."

What's that supposed to mean? Remarkable can go either way — remarkably majestic or remarkably grotesque or, for that matter, anything someone might remark on.

Is she attracted to him? Aimee hasn't shown any interest in a guy since Travis's death. It has to happen sooner or later, I guess, but that vacant, egotistical, pretty-boy kin to our archenemy? What's she thinking?

She takes another bite, chews thoughtfully, and swallows. "You do realize that the fact that Ruby is his sister doesn't mean Yoshi is a bad person."

Aimee always looks for the good in people. I reach into my jar. "I've been researching shifter-on-shifter crimes. It's the big carnivores that are most likely to be killers. No surprise there. But Cats? They're a solid number two after wereorcas."

"Were . . . orcas?" Aimee whispers as the bar manager swings in.

He grabs a blue bandanna from his locker and waves on his way back out.

"Whales usually make their homes on land in coastal

areas or on islands, but if they're at sea too long, it's like they lose themselves to their inner animal. Usually, they hunt fish and other sea animals, but sometimes . . ."

Aimee looks at the gator meat on her fork and sets it down. "They eat sailors?"

A cricket flies from my hand off the table.

Aimee scrambles after it. Chef Nora will have my hide if the thing causes a health-inspection issue. "More like weredolphins, Otters, and Seals." I force myself to my hands and knees under the table. "Some of them are sailors, though, now that you mention it."

"Your point being?" Aimee nudges, scanning the floor.

I'm mostly showing off. She's no fetishist, but it's only natural that she finds shape-shifters fascinating. I'm pretty intrigued by human girls myself. "Cats are bad news. Not as scary as Orcas, but more murderous than Bears or Wolves. They're sneakier, more manipulative. You can't trust them."

"You're prejudiced," Aimee scolds, scooping up the insect. "Did you detect any particular scent to Yoshi's shift? I didn't."

It's an important question, and it says a lot about how shifter-savvy she's become that Aimee is the one to ask it. My werewolf pal Kieren tends to give off pine (like a furry air freshener), and, for no apparent reason, my own transformations stink like rotten eggs. It's embarrassing and probably cost me the phone number of a sexy Raccoon at the last wereteen mixer.

Shaking my head, I brace myself for the pain and push back up. "Yoshi could've used a shower, but that's it."

I reconsider what Aimee said about how easily the Cat retracted his shift. For most of us, shape-changing is a messy, excruciating process. It takes a few minutes, even under the best of circumstances. Apparently, not so with Yoshi, and based on what Travis said about Ruby coming after him in the park, she can morph quickly to Cat form, too.

I warn, "With the Kitaharas, their inner beasts lurk just below the skin." As Aimee exits the break room, I exclaim, "Hey! Where are you going with my cricket?"

"I'm releasing it outside," she informs me. "My heroic gesture for the evening."

YOSHI

I VOLUNTARILY FOLLOW the detectives to the police station. It's a bland, boxy building downtown by the interstate. Several squad cars are parallel parked on bordering streets.

Zaleski and Wertheimer show me upstairs to a spare, fluorescent-lit room, then claim they'll be back after they "take care of a few things."

It's been going on two hours since the detectives bailed, locking the door behind them. I could break out, no problem. But I'm sure the vast majority of cops at the station are human, and it would be catastrophically stupid of me to attract any more attention to myself or do anything else that might out me as a shifter.

58

I'm about to go for it anyway when Zaleski returns with a couple of warm mugs. He takes a seat and gestures at the chair across the table from him.

"Where have you been?" I ask, pacing. "I've been waiting for —"

"Sit," he replies. "I took your meeting with Richards at his warehouse."

Oh. My coffee tastes bitter and watery. "Okay."

As the Bear leans his chair back on its rear legs, I hope it can support his weight. "You really don't know where Ruby is, do you?" he asks.

We've been over this. "No."

"A lot of people believe she was a predator."

He doesn't say "werepredator." I shoot a glance at the surrounding mirrored walls. Maybe I've seen too many cop shows on TV, but I can't help wondering if someone is watching and listening from outside the room.

"Ruby was in 4-H," I tell him. "The two of us worked part-time at our Grams's antiques and bonsai shop. My sister graduated high school second in her class. She came to Austin. . . ." So far, everything I've learned about Ruby's troubles in Austin point to her connection with the late Davidson Morris of Sanguini's. So, what happened to Paxton, the guy who persuaded her to move to town in the first place? The one at the music-promotion agency who supposedly appreciates that she's a Cat?

Zaleski stares at me like he's trying to read my mind.

If I share my last lead with him, will that help or hurt my sister? My instincts tell me that the detective wants to do right. But he wears a badge, and there's no such a thing as fair justice for werepeople. Plus, Clyde mentioned something about Ruby supposedly killing a cop or two.

Zaleski brings the chair down on all fours. "She came to Austin and *what*?"

"Disappeared," I reply. "What did Richards say?"

"Nothing much," the detective admits. "With the families of victims, like Travis's family, they mostly want answers. You know, closure."

Even under the circumstances, I can't help but sympathize. "About my sister . . ."

"I'm doing all I can to find Ruby. But no one has officially reported her as missing, and she hasn't been formally charged with any crime. It's probably smart to leave it that way, at least for now. At the moment, all I've got for her are questions."

Fair enough. "Can I go?"

"You heading home to Kansas?" Zaleski asks.

He'll smell it if I lie. "No."

"Then lay low." He gives me his business card, and now I have two of them. "If you do hear from Ruby, I'd appreciate a heads-up." Zaleski sighs like he knows I'm holding out on him but can't do anything about it. "Otherwise, you're free to go."

I follow him to the elevator. As I hit the button, Wertheimer pops his head out of a doorway down the hall and calls, "Hey, kid! You got somewhere to stay tonight?"

I've slept in my car before. I can do it again. "I'll be all right."

The detectives exchange a look. "No, wait," Zaleski says. "I know a place."

I'm not interested in a youth shelter. I duck into the elevator. "Thanks anyway."

Outside, a couple of homeless guys shuffle by. One is pushing a grocery cart, and the other is singing an old Janis Joplin song. A girl wearing a backpack whizzes past me on a Vespa. Then, up ahead, the shadow I thought was a VW Bug steps onto the sidewalk. It's a werearmadillo in animal form. Outside. In public. Downtown.

I'd say it had balls, but I don't know anything about Armadillo physiology.

It's huge, less cute than I would've imagined, more like a pissed-off armored tank. It's not alone, either. Another Dillo steps in back of me from behind a truck.

I could leap over either one or dart to the side and outrun them. I could —

"Easy, my friends," calls a sixty-something man in a pinstriped business suit, strutting down the middle of the street. "I just want to have a few words with the boy."

61

"If this is about my sister," I begin, "I have no idea —"

"It's about both of you," the approaching man replies, and that's when I notice his revolver. "I'm sure Detective Zaleski has already mentioned that if Ms. Kitahara doesn't turn herself in to me within seventy-two hours, our vendetta against her will extend to include you."

As a matter of fact, Zaleski didn't mention that.

"We're here to make sure you understand that we have the power to follow through on our threat," he explains. "Perhaps you're thinking that as a Cat, you could flee. Or that you could even kill us the way your sister slaughtered my grandson."

Karl Richards, I presume. He's lost his mind. "I'm —"

"Shut up! You may be an über carnivore, but we Dillos prosper in both worlds. We are a proud people with close ties to the Weasels, Rats, and Opossums. We have friends and resources beyond your wildest imagining. You don't know what it is to be hunted until you've been hunted by an Armadillo."

It's hard not to laugh except, again, the gun. Trying to keep in mind what Zaleski had said about grieving families, I decide to take the high ground — literally.

I jump onto the flatbed of the pickup and from there onto the roof of the cab. I show my saber teeth and claws, but keep my face human. "Look, Mr. Richards —"

"To you, I am His Majesty, the werearmadillo king,"

he declares. "And if you give me one more reason to shoot you, I will."

He's got to be bluffing. "So, Your Majesty, you use your exalted power to . . . what?" I reply, recalling his business card. "Regulate in-home climate-control systems? That doesn't sound very regal." Or intimidating.

"Money is power," Richards informs me. "Here in Texas, three-digit summers are scarcely newsworthy. I've made a fortune on air conditioners." He squares his shoulders. "We have commercial and government accounts, too."

Nice. "You're saying it's Ruby or me. Is that all?"

"No," he replies. "You misunderstand. *Both* you and your sister will pay for her assassinating Travis. We will hunt down your every last living relation on this planet, if necessary, adding another to our list every three days. This is war."

Not good. I mean, Grams can take care of herself, and who knows what became of my parents, but . . . "Go play in traffic," I snarl.

Right then two unmarked sedans turn (from opposite ends) onto the one-way street, both flashing police lights. Zaleski and Werthemier jump out with their guns drawn. "Damn it, Richards!" Zaleski shouts. "I thought we had an understanding."

His Majesty slips his weapon into his holster and raises his hands in mock surrender. "We do." He motions to his thugs. They retreat to a black van in the closest pay-parking lot, and the Dillo forms waddle up a short metal ramp into the back.

Zaleski grabs my ankle and yanks me off the truck. "You all right?"

"Yeah," I say, landing neatly on asphalt. "But about a place to stay . . ."

AIMEE

CLYDE AND I ARE TOO WIRED to crash right after work, so Chef Nora invites us to her place to tell the tale about our brush with Ruby's brother. Nora rents out a room in Quincie's art deco house less than five minutes south of Sanguini's.

Because Clyde decides to leave his wheelchair in the SUV, it takes some doing to get him inside and settled at the kitchen table. I'm glad he's making such terrific progress with his physical therapy, but he's pushing too hard. Stubborn Possum.

As Nora serves up mugs of piping-hot cocoa, a knock sounds on the kitchen door.

She bustles over to answer it. "Awfully late for surprise guests."

I follow, hesitating within reach of the knife block on the counter.

Meanwhile, Clyde leans his nose toward the window screen. "It's Zaleski and Yoshi," he announces, breaking the tension.

Nora opens the door and rises on her toes to accept a quick peck on the lips from the detective. "What a nice surprise, hon!" she exclaims.

Clyde and I trade a surprised look that asks, *Since when are they an item?*

Nora has ten to fifteen years on Zaleski. Good for her.

"I left a message on the landline," the detective replies. "You should get a cell phone like everyone else in the world. How do you do business with vendors?"

"During business hours," she says pointedly, extending her hand to Ruby's brother. "I bet you're Yoshi. Welcome to Austin. Come on in out of the cold. I understand that you've already met Clyde and Aimee."

Glaring at the detective, the Cat exclaims, "You didn't tell me *they* lived here!"

"We don't," I reply. "We're just visiting."

"We visit often," Clyde adds from the kitchen table.

"A word, Nora?" Zaleski says, ignoring us. "Upstairs?"

Beyond shifter earshot, he means. They'll probably turn on a faucet and a fan for extra cover. Before leaving,

Nora pours Yoshi some cocoa. When he doesn't accept it right away, she simply sets the mug on the counter and leads the cop out of the room.

On his way out, Zaleski points at Yoshi. "You stay put."

Pushing up to perch on the counter, I can't resist studying Yoshi's smattering of freckles and full lips. Throw in a Cat's grace and the animal magnetism that comes standard with werepredators, and he's the romantic equivalent of a flashing red light.

Yoshi is one of *those* guys. Like my post–eighth-grade summer fling from church camp — Enrique Soto of JV basketball fame. Neither of us noticed the mosquito army ravaging our skin as we cuddled in a docked canoe one night after lights-out.

The next day when he offered me his entire bottle of calamine lotion, I thought that was a sign of true devotion, and it was — for exactly six days and nights of "faith, fellowship, and Christian fun." Then he acted like we were total strangers once the bus crossed back into Austin city limits. It was like we never happened. He was done.

It was just a fling, but I still felt burned and, worse, embarrassed. Thing is, Enrique isn't even my type (I couldn't care less about the respective historical significance of Michael Jordan versus Shaquille O'Neal), but I got sucked in anyway. The abs, the hair, and, to be honest, the fact that someone wanted me, at least for a while. Later, the whole experience only made me appreciate Travis more.

Travis, who was killed by Yoshi's sister.

"Zaleski told me that Ruby has been in this house," the Cat murmurs. "That man she was supposedly dating, Davidson Morris — he lived here."

Yoshi's nostrils flare. He's trying to pick up some trace of his sister's scent. Shape-shifters do that a lot, which makes me paranoid about BO and my period.

"Try outside," Clyde suggests, nodding toward the kitchen door. "She killed Detective Bartok . . . or maybe it was Matthews . . . in the yard. Their partial remains were found in the bushes in back."

"You don't know my sister," Yoshi replies. "You have no right to —"

"She also staked Davidson Morris, who, by the way, was an evil soulless vampire, upstairs on the second floor," I put in. "Not that anyone's complaining," I add in a softer voice. "Good riddance to the bad guy."

"The evil soulless vampire that she'd been screwing," the Possum mutters.

In a blur, Yoshi crosses the room to grab Clyde. "You don't know my sister!"

Oh, hell. Yelling for the grown-ups, I slip down from the counter, draw the biggest carving knife, and point it at Yoshi's back. "Drop the Possum! Now!"

The partially shifted Cat has his claws wrapped around Clyde's neck.

"Don't!" I exclaim. "Please —"

Yoshi tosses Clyde into a bookshelf, knocking off cookbooks, archaeology tomes, and religious texts.

"For heaven's sake!" I drop the cutlery and run past the Cat to my friend. "He can barely walk now."

As I help him up, Clyde grunts. "I told you he was dangerous."

"Then you shouldn't have said that about his sister!" I scold.

As Yoshi returns the butcher knife to the block, Nora and Zaleski storm in. The detective doesn't have his gun drawn, but his fingers hover over the holster.

"It's fine," I announce. "It's over." I take a breath. "They were just being boys."

After a moment to digest that, the chef announces in her not-to-be-disputed voice that Yoshi will be staying with her until further notice, and Zaleski announces in his I'm-going-to-kick-your-ass voice that we're not to tell anyone, or else.

Yoshi breaks the awkward silence that follows by asking me, "What did you mean by 'vampire'? Everybody knows that vamps are extinct."

That *is* what most people think. The last widely rumored sighting of one was in the '60s in Dallas.

"Pfft," Clyde replies.

"Uh . . ." I begin, turning to the adults.

Zaleski suddenly has his pocketknife out and is cleaning his fingernails.

Meanwhile, Nora moves to the refrigerator to take something out. The chef briefly nukes it, adds a dollop of cherry-vanilla ice cream, and then offers it with a fork to the confused Cat. She begins, "This is the kind of news best served over pecan pie."

I half lift, half shove Clyde up behind the wheel of his domino-decked SUV and I'm climbing into the front passenger seat when Yoshi calls, "Aimee, can I talk to you?"

"Don't go," the Possum says. "He's —"

"Enough with the drama," I reply. "I don't love Ruby any more than you do, but Yoshi isn't his sister."

"Cats are tricky," Clyde replies. "Expert liars."

"Two minutes," I promise, hopping back out. "Yoshi's our only lead, remember? He still might be able to help us find Ruby." Once I slam the car door, the Possum hits the high beams, lighting up the driveway.

I jog back to Yoshi. He yawns huge, and it reminds me of big cats at the zoo.

"What is it?" I say, aware that Clyde is watching our every move.

"Less than forty-eight hours ago, I was living the quiet life, restoring my vintage car, romancing country girls, and trying to stay on Grams's good side in Heartland, U.S.A." Yoshi's eyes turn Cat-like, pupils wide. "Since then, I've had multiple firearms and a knife pointed at me, been

70

twice provoked by a scrawny, passive-aggressive Possum, had my life threatened by the werearmadillo king, and —"

"Threatened?" I echo. "By Pop-Pop Richards?" I've attended a handful of family events with Travis, plus the funeral, and that's what his grandfather insists I call him.

A prolonged honk comes from Clyde's SUV.

Yoshi shakes his head. "Forget it. This is my problem. I'll —"

"Just spit it out," I say.

"If Ruby doesn't turn up soon, the Armadillos will be gunning for me, too. They want revenge and lots of it. I need to find out what really happened and fast. I doubt that Zaleski told me everything. You might. Besides, I could use a local guide."

"In exchange for what?" I ask. "Why should I help you help a known . . ." I almost say "killer." That's the word Clyde would use — or worse. "Fugitive?"

"According to what Zaleski told me, Ruby hasn't been formally charged," Yoshi replies, pacing on the driveway. "Nobody's going to miss a homicidal bloodsucker like Davidson Morris." He pauses like it's still an effort to process that information. "But if that werebear detective was convinced that my sister murdered a teenage shifter and a couple of cops, don't you think he'd put out an APB on her?"

Hmm. The extraordinarily sexy werecat has a point.

"Look," Yoshi begins again. "We both want to find Ruby. I get that you're upset about what happened to your friend. Maybe you're all looking too hard for someone to blame. I'm sure the Possum is. But I know she's not guilty, and I'll prove it to you."

Clyde's horn goes ballistic, and an upstairs light in the neighbor's house comes on.

Yoshi hisses in his general direction, and it's time to bail.

Glancing at the idling SUV, I reply, "Tell you what: Sanguini's is closed on Sundays. How about we meet here tomorrow morning? I'll answer your questions if you answer mine."

CLYDE

"WHAT WAS ALL THAT ABOUT?" I demand as Aimee buckles her seat belt. "I want to hear every detail. Every little thing. What did Yoshi say?"

"Would the Dillos really kill Yoshi for something Ruby did?" she asks in reply.

Travis is (was?) my best friend (when you're talking about ghosts, tense is difficult), but I'm no expert on the inner workings of werearmadillo culture.

"Unclear," I say, backing slowly out of the driveway. "They could just be trying to lure her out, using the brother as bait, and since when are you on Yoshi's side?"

"What do you mean?" Aimee asks, turning up the heater. "I'm not on his side."

"You yelled at me in front of him in the kitchen!" I exclaim as we turn onto the dead-end street. "Now you're more worried about him than finding Travis's killer."

As I brake at the stop sign, she says, "I yelled at you because you started that ridiculous display of testosterone, talking trash about Yoshi's sister. Of course I want Ruby questioned. Ruby, not Yoshi. He wasn't even in Texas —"

"That we know of," I point out, making a mental note that Aimee said "questioned" and not "punished." That's Yoshi's doing. She wasn't alone with him for three minutes, and he's already spun her mind.

"Fine," she agrees. "That we know of. But the Dillos have supposedly threatened to extend the price they've put on Ruby's head to him. Assuming he's not at fault, Yoshi shouldn't be the one to pay. That would be wrong, Clyde, horribly wrong, and besides, Travis's true killer would get off free. You tell me: is that justice?"

I like Aimee. I do. But she's always obsessing over some cause, and besides, there's nothing I hate more than arguing with someone who's making more sense than me.

I head south on Congress Avenue, cruising by the 1950s motels, the costume shop, Sanguini's, and the Tex-Mex restaurant. "What else did Yoshi want to talk to you about?"

"What do you think?" Aimee says. "Finding Ruby, making sure she's safe. He's concerned about her, which is only natural. It also suggests that he's a decent guy."

74

I snort. "You like him. You think he's hot."

As I swing into the Bouldin Creek neighborhood, Aimee stares out her window, ignoring me. Within a block, the landscape changes to a mix of new construction and small cottages, some of which are decorated with holiday lights year-round.

Once I put the SUV in park outside her apartment, she replies, "I don't even know him." That's when I realize she's seriously pissed. "How superficial do you think I am?" Aimee goes on. "News flash: being in the presence of a robust-looking male in no way shuts down my capacity for rational thought."

"Robust?" I reply. Do *I* look robust? What does *robust* mean, anyway?

Aimee gets out and marches off without bothering to close the passenger door behind her. I unbuckle my seat belt and wince as I stretch to reach it.

Someday, I will learn when to shut up.

AIMEE

I WAKE TO THE ELECTRONIC CHIME of my mother's laptop. At least Mom didn't try to rouse me for church. I usually work until close on weekends, but over winter break I've been going in every night to make some extra cash.

Dad hasn't paid child support since he took that tech job in Hong Kong, or, at least, he keeps claiming there's a persistent glitch in his bank's direct-deposit system.

My mom is a former Pottery Barn manager, trying to remake herself as a life coach. She still works part-time as a sales clerk at Barton Creek Square Mall and is talking about going back to school to study psychology. Meanwhile, our employee-discounted furniture is awesome.

I rise from the foldout sofa bed and, yawning, mosey down the hall.

At her bedroom door, I begin, "Mind if I take a rain check today?" We'd been planning to hit a Jimmy Stewart movie marathon. "Something has come up with —"

"Your friends?" she asks, pivoting in the desk chair. "Again?"

Before I can reply, Mom adds, "Forget I said that." She straightens. "I have friends of my own. Being a mother is important to me, but I won't stoop to guilt trips or model to you that a woman is incomplete without a man and children to define her."

Uh-huh. "New self-help book?"

She holds up a copy of *The Single Mother's Guide to Raising Herself.* "Am I becoming that predictable?"

I laugh. "I find it charming."

Sounding more like her usual self, she asks, "Are you off with Clyde?"

"Not exactly," I reply, sitting on the corner of the bed. "There's this boy. He's visiting from Kansas." Kansas has a nice, wholesome connotation. "His name is Yoshi, and he's staying with Nora."

"Is he cute?" Mom asks.

"More than cute," I confess, recalling the fit of his jeans. "More like smoldering."

YOSHI

LAST NIGHT WHEN ZALESKI ANNOUNCED I'd be staying with his "lady friend," I wondered if he might actually trust me. Then I realized that he was spending the night, too. Today I wake up in the cluttered attic to the aroma of Nora's promised chicken-fried steak and eggs Benedict, and the world smells brighter.

There has to be a rational explanation for the allegations against Ruby. She's probably in hiding somewhere safe, waiting for everything to blow over. Today I'll do my damnedest to find her and straighten it all out.

I pull my jeans back on and rummage through the T-shirts that Nora left stacked for me on a nearby rocking chair. I pick a black short-sleeved one that spells COEXIST out of the religious symbols of various faiths.

Standing in front of the mirrored door to an antique wardrobe, I'm combing my hair when the reflection of a stack of boxes labeled DM catches my eye.

DM as in Davidson Morris? It's got to be.

With a glance at the empty stairwell, I cross the attic and dig in. The contents are a jumble — toiletries, old checkbooks, Hawaiian shirts — like someone tossed everything in without bothering to sort through it first.

"Yoshi!" Nora calls from downstairs. "Grub's on!"

"Coming!" I reply. I'm about to give up and sneak back later when a red envelope catches my eye. I pull out a birthday card with a coffin pictured on the front, the trim lined in real red felt. I don't get the punch line on the inside, but the return address is for Ruby Kitahara.

Jackpot! I shove the envelope in my pocket and return the boxes to their approximate original positions.

"It's getting cold!" Nora calls again.

Two staircases later, I gratefully accept a nearly overflowing plate. (The crispy hash browns go a long way to soaking up the hollandaise sauce.)

Nora says that she already shooed out Zaleski and invites me to church.

"No, thanks." I wipe my mouth with a napkin. "I've got . . ." Should I tell her that I'm off to track Ruby? Won't she relay anything I say to Zaleski? "A date."

"A date?" Nora cocks her head. "My, you move fast! Didn't you hit town only yesterday?"

"Aimee," I say. "It's not a *date* date. We're just going to hang out."

Nora and I make small talk over breakfast. It's a relief to finally meet someone in this town who seems genuinely glad to get to know me. She even knows a werewolf who spent a night in Grams's barn last fall. Small world, I guess.

After mentioning that she's Sanguini's third and latest chef, Nora answers my question before I can ask it. "I've never met Ruby. She wasn't there long and took off before my time."

"Everyone talks like she's a monster," I say.

Nora's smile is gentle. "I've known my share of monsters and even found it in my heart to love a couple of them." She clears my plate. "You strike me as a good boy. This morning I'll put in a prayer request for you and your sister."

Aimee shows up on foot about five minutes after Nora leaves for services. I'm sitting on the hood of my car, scrolling through old text messages, looking for clues.

I'm amused that Aimee thinks fifty-something degrees is chilly. She's sporting a green fleece jacket with a long matching scarf. It brings out the green in her hair.

"Where's your boyfriend?" I ask. "I half expected him to tag along today."

"Who, Clyde?" Aimee asks with a quirk of her lips. "We're just friends."

Best news I've heard in days. She's swiped translucent gel onto her brows and lashes, baby-pink gel onto her lips. I wonder if that's normal for her or an extra effort.

I have my share of experience with human girls — more than my fair share. But none of them knew I'm a Cat. Somehow the fact that Aimee knows changes everything. I'm not playing pretend. I've got no choice but to be the whole, real Yoshi.

I slide off the hood and inform her that Ruby moved to Austin to work as a music-promotion intern with a guy named Paxton. "Later, we can hit some clubs, ask around."

"Does this Paxton have a last name?" Aimee asks.

Reaching into my back pocket, I shake my head. "That would be too easy, but he's supposedly sympathetic to werepeople rights. . . . He might be attached to the local urban scene." I wonder how tapped in she is, beyond her Possum "just" friend. It's a big deal, confiding shifter heritage to a human — forbidden, for the most part.

"We've got all day," Aimee says. "Any other bright ideas?"

Either I trust her or not. "Just one," I reply, pulling out the red envelope. I unfold it and show her the return address. "Can you take me here?"

"Hmm." Aimee studies Ruby's loopy handwriting and then puts her palm out. "It's not far. Give me your keys."

AIMEE

STEERING HIS PRECIOUS CAR NORTH on Congress and then west, I don't mention to Yoshi that I've only had my driver's license for a few months. Or that I failed the test the first two times I took it.

I'm familiar with Ruby's high-end apartment complex. It's located near married-student housing and the city golf course. I've passed it a million times on my way to have fruit tarts and iced tea with my mom on the lake.

As we cruise by Auditorium Shores, I explain that Ruby was leading a double life, pretending to be a living vampire.

Rolling down the passenger-side window, Yoshi asks, "What's that?"

I take a breath. "A human being who drinks blood from virgin donors." The way I see it, what consenting adults do on full-moon nights in Hill Country caves is their own business. Cruising toward Lake Austin Boulevard, I add, "There's a whole subculture built around it." According to the waiters, a handful of living vampires are among Sanguini's regular customers. They dress gorgeously and tip even better.

"Kinky," Yoshi replies. "Why would a Cat do such a thing?"

I'm not sure how much to tell him. A few minutes later, I pull the car up to the apartment key code/com system and finally say, "We think Ruby playacted to attract Davidson Morris so she could spy on him and his vamp buddies. By pretending to be a wannabe, Ruby convinced them that she sincerely wanted to be turned."

He raises his eyebrows. "You're saying my sister was some kind of secret agent?"

"And assassin," I put in. "She staked Davidson Morris, remember?"

I dial the office and ask to be let in.

As the gate electronically retracts, Yoshi asks, "Working for . . . ?"

"The Cats?" I guess, mostly fishing. It's the assumption we've been going on, but there's not much meat to it. According to Clyde, Cats don't have any form of organized government. They're too independent for that.

Once I cut the engine, Yoshi says, "I don't need you for this."

Oh, please. "I'm not going to wait in the car."

"What if we find something that leads us to Ruby?" he asks. "Your buddy Clyde has already made up his marsupial mind. The Armadillo king is ready to play executioner, the facts be damned. How do I know you won't turn in Ruby to the Dillos —?"

"I won't." I get out of the car. "I wouldn't. I want the truth, too."

Yoshi joins me in the parking lot. "That's not good enough."

"I owe Ruby my life," I admit. "Probably my soul, too."

He flares his nostrils, trying to smell out a lie. "You? How —?"

"Long story," I say, heading toward the stucco-and-limestone management office. When Yoshi stays put, I glance over my shoulder. "I'm sorry, but I don't know you well enough to tell you about it. If we could become friends, it would be different."

"We can't become friends?" There's a trace of hurt in his voice. "Why not?"

"Travis was my boyfriend," I snap. "Well, almost. Just leave it, okay?"

He does.

Our cover story is that Yoshi is shopping for a lease. Not hugely original, but it gets us in. We pick up a couple of brochures and chat up the receptionist about the fitness center and laundry facilities. Fortunately, the salesperson is occupied with another prospective tenant.

We thank the receptionist and excuse ourselves, making noises about checking out the pool. The complex is huge, made up of eight separate four-story buildings, painted off-white with brown trim. It's about five years old, in an affluent neighborhood, convenient to downtown, Mopac, and the lake.

We find Building F on the far side of the property.

"Are you from family money?" I ask, figuring a music-promotion internship, assuming it paid at all, wouldn't be lucrative enough for Ruby to cover the rent.

"Not so much," Yoshi replies as we march up the outside staircase.

He hesitates at the door of apartment F409, Ruby's apartment, and we exchange a ready-for-anything look. Yoshi knocks, waits a minute, checks to make sure no one's around, and then shoves the door open, breaking the lock.

"Hello?" he calls. "Ruby?"

No answer. No alarm, either. It must be nice to have super strength.

I follow him in. The unit is a one-bedroom—beige

walls and carpeting — with a living-dining area, bathroom, and kitchenette. "The electricity has been turned off."

He tries the sink. "The water, too."

I do a quick sweep, mostly to reassure myself that the apartment is unoccupied.

"Hurry," Yoshi urges. "The cops may be watching the place."

"The Dillos, too," I say. I can't believe I'm in Ruby's apartment. If Clyde finds out, he'll be furious that I didn't bring him along. Not to mention that I'm here with Yoshi.

The apartment apparently came furnished in durable earth-tone fabrics. Ruby's clothes still hang in the closet and overstuff the hamper and lie in clumps on the bedroom carpet. Her bountiful collection of sparkly cosmetics and toiletries clutters the medicine-cabinet shelves. She left a half-stocked fridge, too. The eggs have gone bad, along with the milk, fruits, and veggies. It smells awful, no doubt worse to Yoshi.

He shuts the refrigerator door fast.

When I open a kitchen cabinet filled with brown rice, pistachios, and cereal boxes, a dozen tiny beige moths fly out.

"Ruby hasn't been back here in a while," Yoshi muses, crossing the apartment. "If she hasn't paid in as long, she's far enough behind on the rent to be evicted. So, why hasn't this place been cleaned out? Leased to someone else?"

"The economy?" I guess. "Maybe they have several

other units identical to this one available, or maybe they're hoping Ruby will come back, or . . ." I recall my parents' latest tiff over finances. "She might be paid up — sending checks from who-knows-where or having the money automatically transferred each month from a bank account." I suspect that Zaleski and Wertheimer know the answer.

In the bedroom doorway, Yoshi is holding up a black leather corset with black lace trim and red satin ties. "Good luck fitting into that," I tease.

"My sister wore things like this in public," he mutters like it just sank in. "There's hardly anything else in the closet except her clothes from home, shoved to the back."

"Do you smell anyone?" I ask. "Besides Ruby, I mean."

Yoshi lifts his nose. "Human, but it's off somehow."

"Probably the vampire," I say. "From what I hear, it's a sort of echo scent."

"And another Cat," Yoshi adds. "But that's somehow strange, too." He tosses the corset onto the sofa and returns to the bedroom.

A high-school yearbook on the coffee table catches my eye. I open it to the section on the senior class and find Ruby's photo in the *K*s.

I've seen pictures of her before, of course. Clyde has shown me. She exudes slinky sauciness — every inch the kind of woman who could seriously rock a leather corset.

In her school photo, Ruby looks sweet, not sex

kittenish. Without the severe makeup or the skunk stripe in her dark hair, she's a different girl.

At Waterloo High, my green highlights and tats are no big deal, but it's all relative. I would've stood out as much at this small-town Kansas school as Ruby did here in Austin (even at Sanguini's). Paging back, I find Yoshi's picture — that irresistible smile — and then check the index. Neither Kitahara sibling appears except in their class photos. No science club, no homecoming court or sports teams. Like most werepeople, they kept a low profile — possibly lower than most, given the size of their school and hometown.

Ruby kept her yearbook handy. Did she miss the life she left behind?

I hear a soft "Oh" from the other room and put the book down. "What is it?" I ask, joining Yoshi in the bedroom.

Glancing up from the nightstand drawer, he grimaces. "I can deal with the fact that my sister is no longer a virgin. But I in no way needed to know that she's into flavored glow-in-the-dark condoms." He runs a hand through his dark hair. "It makes no sense."

Overwhelmed by the awkwardness of the situation, I begin channeling my mother. "Condoms not only prevent pregnancy, they're also helpful in combatting the transmission of—"

"That's not what I meant." Yoshi shuts the drawer. "Condoms are worn by men."

I reject a couple of possibilities before replying, "Everybody knows that."

He crosses his arms over his chest. "Didn't everybody know Ruby's into girls?"

I sure didn't. "Since when?"

The Cat shrugs. "Based on the collection of vintage Diana Rigg–as–Emma Peel posters hanging in her bedroom at Grams's, I'd say, since forever."

So Yoshi's sister morphed from a gay, small-town sweetheart to a bitchy, big-city hetero (or at least bi) seductress-assassin. No wonder he's confused. "Why don't I take the bedroom and bath?" I suggest, feeling protective of Ruby's privacy, or at least Yoshi's sensibilities. "You search the rest of the apartment."

I discover that Ruby stashed a silky blindfold and a set of handcuffs in the lower drawer of the nightstand. I leave them there. I also leave the discarded black thong under the bed and the collection of Kama Sutra oils on the bathroom windowsill.

I'm completely unqualified to get a read on any of this. The only boy I've more than kissed was Enrique. It wasn't that huge of a deal, but he does know that I wear a padded bra. I never kissed Travis. He was shy. I was gun-shy.

Not that it's helping to dwell on it now.

Ruby has a passion for self-help paperbacks that reminds me of my mother — the self-help part anyway, not the specific topics. Under discarded clothes, on the toilet tank, and in the corner of her chaotic closet, I come across titles like *Leather, Metal, and Other Aphrodisiacs* and *Love Yourself: Batteries Optional.*

Moving on, I discover that Ruby wore cinnamon musk and burned sandalwood incense. She tucked a black-and-white snapshot of herself and Yoshi into the mirror over her dresser. They were about nine and eleven years old, and they'd posed, cheek to cheek, facing the camera, with their cheeks puffed out, blowing paper party horns.

I occasionally peek in on him, searching beneath couch cushions or under the kitchen sink. We've left dozens of fingerprints. We should've worn gloves.

I'm feeling between the mattresses when I hear something slam and rush to investigate. A cabinet door is swinging from the top hinge, and Yoshi's shaking his hand.

"What happened?" I ask. "Did the kitchen cabinet mock your hair?"

Yoshi faces me, gripping the granite counter behind him. He broke the skin on his knuckles. "I'm no detective," he says. "This is ridiculous. I feel like a goddamned werewolf, sniffing around."

Is Yoshi usually a hothead — an unsettling quality in anyone, but especially a werepredator — or is it his fear for his sister making him act this way? "Focus," I say.

Nodding, he pulls one of the drawers completely out and sets it on the table.

"Have you gone through these old receipts?" I ask, moving in to take a closer look.

There are a lot of them, mostly crumpled. I begin smoothing out each one in turn. Most came from boring places like the grocery store or gas station.

"Ruby spent a fortune on dry cleaning alone," Yoshi says, batting at a little beige moth. "I can't imagine how she afforded any of this."

"She never pulled a paycheck at Sanguini's," I reply, "but Davidson Morris had been giving her money for a while." That sounded sleazier than I meant it to.

Yoshi holds up a faded receipt. "Enlightenment Alley. Do you know it?"

"It's a shop off Anderson Lane," I reply, brightening. "The owner . . ."

"What about him?"

"Paxton!" I exclaim. "He has a college-age son by the same name."

"Shh!" Yoshi goes still. "Someone's coming. We should go."

"Without being spotted?" I ask in a low voice. "How? There's only one way out."

"And I busted the lock," he says. "They can come in without a key."

Yoshi slips the shop receipt into his jeans pocket, takes my hand, leads me across the living room into Ruby's bedroom, and locks that door behind us. Then he unlatches the one window that doesn't open to the front of the apartment.

"Are you crazy?" I ask, gauging the drop. "We're on the fourth floor. I'm a human being, remember? I don't heal like a shifter."

Yoshi shoves the window open wide. "That's why we're going up." He ducks through, straddling the sill, and offers his hand again. "Do you trust me?"

Trust him? I wasn't even willing to let him drive.

From the living room, I hear a man with a slight Mexican accent. Whoever it is has already come inside and started pounding on the bedroom door. "Ruby?"

Yoshi swings all the way out the window, grabbing onto who-knows-what for support. "Come on!" he urges. "Wrap your arms around me. Hurry!"

I latch on to his neck and hook my legs around his waist, hyper aware of the intimacy of our embrace. Using a gutter downspout for balance, Yoshi launches us up and grasps the roofline. A short, pained breath escapes him.

I whisper, "You all right?"

"Shouldn't have punched the cabinet," he replies through gritted teeth.

Yoshi takes a deeper breath and then raises us both to the top. We land in a heap on our sides in each other's arms. Scared as I am, it feels good.

"Ruby!" the man shouts out the window. "Ruby, we can help you!"

I try to catch a glimpse of the intruder, but Yoshi holds me in place.

After a while, we hear Ruby's front door shut. We crawl across the roof to peer over the parking lot. Below, a middle-aged Latino priest and a teenage guy large enough to wrestle professionally climb into a light-blue van and drive away. Appearances can be deceiving, but they don't look like bad guys. I ask, "Is Ruby Catholic?"

Yoshi rubs his forehead. "She wasn't when she left Kansas."

CLYDE

I BLEW IT YESTERDAY with Yoshi. We faced off, eye to eye, man to man, Opossum to Cat. Which begs the question: What was I thinking, trying to use dominance against him?

Don't get me wrong. I'm not about to project "prey shifter," but I went too far the other way. I went against my better instincts, against everything I know about the food chain. It was also self-defeating. I made a total idiot out of myself in front of Aimee, and for what? I didn't learn one thing about Ruby in the process. And to think how I've been strutting around, talking large about battling evil-doers in the name of justice.

Who am I trying to kid? I'm Clyde Leonard Gilbert, a dishwashing, babysitting sophomore marsupial. It's so freaking unfair.

Wolves and Cats get all the girls. They get all the glory. They don't fail their dead best friends.

The mystery of the day? On her way home from church, Nora texted me, asking that I meet her at this abandoned construction site. I'm looking at a five-story metal-beam shell beside a huge asphalt parking lot, hidden from view of the steady traffic on Mopac by hills and trees. Nora asked that I come alone.

I don't have long to chat. Aimee is stopping by later to help me take care of the quads while my parents "make an appearance" at a wererat retirement brunch.

Leaning against my SUV, I say, "I feel like I should know a code word."

Nora gives me a hug. "How're you feeling, Clyde? You really up to taunting strange werepredators in my kitchen?"

"I'm sorer this morning than I was yesterday." I lift my leg, testing for flexibility. "I've tried to shift a couple of times. If I can make it all the way to full Possum, my human form might reboot when I turn back."

What I don't say is that any effort to transform hurts like a mother, and I don't want to try it on painkillers or muscle relaxants. Wereopposums don't stress over controlling our animal form the same way that Wolves or Bears or, for that matter, Cats do. Unless we're cornered, our response to conflict is usually to bolt or play dead. But nobody likes to lose it. I have nightmares about showing tail in the boys' locker room at school.

"You're growing up," Nora says, opening her car trunk. "Getting yourself into all kinds of trouble." She pulls out shiny silver crutches.

"I have a pair at home," I tell her. The crutches are supposed to be the step between the chair and walking normally again, assuming I ever can walk normally again.

The chair has dignity. Professor X has a wheelchair. Captain Pike has a wheelchair. A cane could be cool, especially a sword cane.

But the crutches just make my armpits ache.

Nora holds them out. "Humor me."

I don't usually let people boss me around, but Nora is the top chef in the state — maybe the country — and I work in her kitchen. Besides, her previous employer was a world-renowned undead badass. Under that homespun exterior beats the heart of a spatula-wielding warrior woman.

I make a show of using the crutches to swing around the parking lot.

"You need practice." Nora gestures to a Dumpster about a hundred feet away. "Now, point one of those bad boys at that and squeeze the handgrip three times, quickly."

One, two, three — suddenly, crackling blue energy blasts from the tip. My arm flails up from the recoil and so does the charge. "Whoa!"

I hit pavement, let go, and it's over.

"Enchanted or engineered?" I ask, gasping.

Nora offers me a hand up. "Both. Pump four times for a lethal charge — something that can level a hellhound. Three is enough to stun practically anyone with a living soul."

"Is this because Yoshi's in town?" I add, struggling to my feet. "I thought you liked him." At least well enough to feed him and put a roof over his head.

"I do," the chef replies. "But even the finest folks can be dangerous if they're pushed too far. You may have the heart of a lion, Clyde, but you need a way to defend yourself. These are the latest model. Watch out for glitches, and use them only in case of an emergency."

YOSHI

ENLIGHTENMENT ALLEY IS LOCATED in a quirky outdoor mall about ten minutes north of downtown. I note the dine-in movie theater. The sushi restaurant. The martial arts studio and the herb store. The economy is better here than in Kansas.

"The priest claimed he wanted to help Ruby," Aimee remarks as we cross an arched wooden bridge over a lily pond. "Maybe we should have talked to him."

"What if he was lying?" I reply. "We don't even know if he's really a priest."

She has a point, though. I've got to watch out for my flight instinct. It's stronger in Cats than most were-predators. If I realized earlier that Ruby's home invaders were a guy dressed like a priest and an overgrown kid, I might've taken a chance on them.

The Enlightenment Alley storefront is not on an alley. It is a gleaming kaleidoscope of colors. Crystals hang from almost-invisible wires behind the glass, reflecting sunlight in a dizzying rainbow array.

Inside, I'm hit hard by the aroma of smudge and scented candles, the gurgle of dozens of wall and tabletop fountains.

"This is a gift shop?" I mutter.

"A New Age gift shop," Aimee explains.

I note the wind chimes. The political bumper stickers. The poster celebrating endangered animals. Handmade signs point to "After Solstice Sale" items. I identify tiny speakers mounted in the corners of the ceiling as the source of croaking, chirping, and rustling noises. Confirming that they're artificial helps squash my urge to give chase.

"Groovy," I reply. It's the word Grams would use.

I shoot a glance at the balding guy in the nearest plush chair. He's reading up on Hinduism. Or what passes for Hinduism in a place like this.

Aimee gently elbows me in the ribs. "My mom and I come here all the time."

The bookshelf labels include: HARMONY, COURAGE, ALTERNATIVE MEDICINE, NATURAL HEALING, SPIRITUAL, PSYCHIC POWER, YOGA, MASSAGE, ASTROLOGY, and PERSONAL GROWTH.

"Seriously?" I ask, pointing to the UFO section.

"You might try being more open-minded," Aimee suggests. "There was a time when most people thought shape-shifters were mythological."

I hold up *Massage for Lovers*. "Redundant, don't you think?"

Aimee blushes to her blond roots. She's definitely a virgin.

I haven't considered before that a human could be knowingly attracted to a shifter as more than an exotic or in a fetish kind of way. But Aimee was, if not in love, then at least in like with the deceased Armadillo prince.

Plus, a Dillo? A beady-eyed, thick-bodied *werearmadillo*? She's not a superficial girl, and superficial romances are the only kind I've ever had.

Aimee skims the spines on the "Angels" shelf.

"What?" she demands. "You're staring."

I can't help myself. "Do you really believe in this stuff?" I ask. "Are you all that religious?"

Her smile is oddly serene. "More like spiritual, but I know what I know."

I follow her across the store. The clerk is costumed like some kind of priestess, complete with gray lipstick and a flowing silver hooded cloak.

"Talk about living the cliché," I whisper.

She recognizes Aimee as a regular. "Welcome back!"

"You look positively folkloric!" Aimee exclaims as we reach the jewelry case.

"Thank you, thank you!" the clerk replies, stepping back to spin for inspection. She has long snow-white hair. "I'm playing the White Witch this season in *The Lion, the Witch, and the Wardrobe* at the children's theater."

That'll teach me not to make assumptions.

The clerk hands Aimee a promotional flyer. "This afternoon will be our last performance. How was your holiday? How's your mama?"

Aimee introduces her as Sandra. They visit a while, and I'm getting impatient when Aimee asks, "Is Paxton around?"

"Paxton Senior and the missus are out of the country," Sandra replies. "Shopping their way through Dubai. Paxton Junior is working days over winter break in the mail room at the law firm and . . ." She glances past us. "Excuse me a sec."

Sandra comes around the counter to assist a customer.

A framed certificate hangs on the wall. It proclaims Sandra an honors graduate of a taxidermy school. That doesn't seem to fit with her image, but this is Texas. Probably even earth mothers hunt here. "Ask her about Ruby," I whisper.

"Breathe," Aimee replies. "Go look at the CDs."

I run a hand through my hair. "All I want —"

"Let me handle this. If you act all intense, she'll get suspicious."

I reluctantly wander to the racks of CDs. The labels read: WOOD FLUTES, CHANTING MONKS, AMBIENT, MEDITATION, HEALING, and NONPROFIT. I curl the hand that still aches from having punched the cabinet. Aimee gave me a squeeze of antiseptic lotion from her purse to clean it, and the broken skin on my knuckles has already scabbed over.

It's not like me to lose my temper like that. Then again, my sister's life isn't usually on the line. Neither is mine, for that matter.

To cheer myself up, I check out Aimee's cute hind end. When she shifts her weight, I take a sharp breath and choke on the scent of eucalyptus.

She glances back. "You all right?"

I nod, cough, and plop down on a beanbag beneath the wind chimes.

Probably as an excuse to linger, Aimee fills out an entry form for a chance to win dinner for two at Thai Garden. According to the sign, the menu is vegan and gluten free.

When Sandra returns, Aimee asks to take a peek at a yin-yang pendant in the case. "You know," she begins, "I thought I spotted Paxton Junior at Sanguini's a few months back. He was out with a petite woman. Asian with long —"

"That must've been Ruby," Sandra cuts in, setting the necklace on the glass countertop. "Saucy little thing, if you get my meaning. I haven't seen her in months, and as far as I know, he hasn't, either."

For the next few minutes, Aimee tries to finagle more information out of Sandra to no avail. That's all we get. I have to admit, I'm more than a little disappointed.

On our way out, Aimee snags an orange flyer off the store bulletin board.

Studying the photo, I say, "This is a Bear band with some kind of Cat woman doing vocals." Even in human form, Bears are easy to spot by body type. With Cats, it's more subtle. How we move or, in the case of a photo, how we hold ourselves. The lead singer is too tall for a female of my specific breed. Beats me if she's a werelion or Liger or part human, but she's definitely smokin'. I'd love to make that kitty purr.

As Aimee and I once again cross the arched bridge over the lily pond, I ask, "Do we know where the law firm is? What it's called?"

"Tornquist and Eastwick." She does a quick search on her phone. "P. Tornquist is also the name of the owner of a local music-promotion company."

Bingo.

AIMEE

JUST PAST THE WINDSOR EXIT, I'm about to check a text from Clyde when Detective Wertheimer pulls the car over. He ducks in Yoshi's backseat like he's worried someone might see us talking. "Well, well, well," Wertheimer begins. "When did you two become such good friends?"

"Is there a problem, officer?" Yoshi asks, turning off the radio.

"Don't play dumb, kid," he replies. "Me and Zaleski told you to lay low, not prance around town, playing Nancy Drew with —"

"We're not playing," I say, though the Nancy Drew part is flattering.

"You've been tailing us," Yoshi states. "I spotted you two exits ago."

"No kidding." The detective leans closer. "I wanted to warn you. Watch out for the Tornquists. They've got deep pockets, and Daddy T is well connected."

"Did you question him about Ruby?" Yoshi asks.

"The younger Mr. Tornquist came in voluntarily," Wertheimer explains. "However, he chose to do so without any advance notice while Zaleski and I were away on a cruise retreat. A couple of other cops talked to him."

Yoshi adjusts the rearview mirror. "Human cops?"

Wertheimer doesn't take the bait, but I know what they're both thinking. Many werepeople can gauge others' emotions — fear, aggression, even passion. Even better, most can ID the species of fellow shifters by scent.

Or, as Travis used to joke, "The nose knows."

Silence fills the car until Wertheimer finally relaxes. "So far as we've been able to figure, Tornquist isn't guilty of anything except being your sister's ex-boyfriend." He rubs his eyelids. "We don't even know for sure if they were romantically involved. But . . ."

"But what?" I ask.

Wertheimer clears his throat. "Several Austinites have been classified as missing over the past few months. We have a partial handle on what happened there."

"Vampires," I inform Yoshi. "Including the one Ruby staked."

Wertheimer scowls at me for mentioning it (police cover-up) but goes on, "The number of total missing is higher than reported."

"Because the rest of the missing people are shifters," Yoshi suggests. "Their loved ones are less likely to go to the cops, at least through regular channels."

"Vamps strongly prefer humans over werepeople for food," I say. "And shifters can't be cursed with their blood to become neophytes. This must be someone, something else that's targeting the local wereperson population."

"Which is why we all need to be extra careful," Wertheimer concludes. "Yoshi, you scamper back to Nora's, flip on ESPN, kick up your kitty heels, and let me and Zaleski find your sister. If you want to woo the young lady, do it out of sight."

Does he mean me? Am I the one being wooed?

"I'm not big on turning tail," Yoshi replies. "But I'll take it under advisement."

"See that you do." With that, the detective exits the car.

Yoshi starts the ignition. "Cops go on cruise retreats?"

I smile at the idea of Wertheimer sipping a mai tai in an aloha shirt, cargo shorts, and flip-flops. "What kind of shifter do you think he is?"

Clyde and I have spent quality time pondering the question, but it's always felt rude to ask Wertheimer directly, especially since he isn't officially "out" in that way to us.

"Can't tell," Yoshi says, continuing south. "Which, given the long list of werepeople who've crashed a night or two in Grams's barn over the years . . . He's either a rare species, one I've never come across before or, possibly, a Wild Card."

"A Wild Card?" I prompt.

"For a Cat and a Lion or, say, a Wolf and a Coyote to have cubs . . . They're so closely related, it's no big deal." Yoshi lowers his visor. "But if you're talking about two very different animal forms — like a Moose and a Boar, for example, either their offspring default to human-form only or they can alternate at will between human and the two animal forms. That's what we call a Wild Card. They're much harder to ID by scent."

I've never thought about it before, what happens when radically different shifters have kids. Then again, it was such a huge deal when Travis invited me into his world. I was reluctant to seem too curious. I let him share what he wanted when he wanted, and I have a general idea of how they all evolved, from the Ice Age on, living in seclusion or at least in secret. But so much is still a mystery to me.

"About Tornquist . . ." I yank the band flyer out of my pocket and read: " 'Jazz Man Bookings presents Fayard and the French Horns.' That's Tornquist's promotion company, and the group plays tonight at a club on Lavaca Street. If Junior is babysitting his daddy's businesses, it's possible he'll show."

YOSHI

I'M HUNGRY AGAIN. Weremammals have higher metabolisms than humans. Teenage males have higher metabolisms than anyone else on earth. I'm always hungry.

Aimee joins me at a bright-yellow picnic table set in an otherwise empty lot alongside a silver food trailer where dolled-up cupcakes are sold. She's bought a six-pack mix of chocolate, vanilla, and mango passion. The icing is swirled and dotted with multicolored sprinkles.

"I've been thinking about the Dillos' potential price on your head," she says. "It's very Han Solo. I mean, not yet, because they're still hoping to —"

"Kill my sister?" I hand Aimee a napkin. "Sorry, I think there was a compliment in there somewhere." I cock my head, studying her. "I've been trying to figure you out. Are you a geek girl, a Goth girl, or a New-Age hippie girl?"

"Can't I be all three?" she replies, self-consciously touching her neck tattoo.

"Not in Kansas," I joke.

"Well, this is Austin." She goes for the mango passion. "I'm an Aimee, an individual. Do you usually categorize girls based on first impressions?"

"Everybody, not just girls," I admit. "That's all I've got time for."

"Aren't you a small-town guy?" she asks. "I mean, you're not from Kansas City, right? Or Wichita? I thought small-town people knew everything about each other."

It's interesting that Aimee thinks she knows something about Kansas. Pretty much everything I thought about Texas is bogus, based on my visit so far. "I'm more of a country boy. Ruby and I were homeschooled until high school. By then, everyone had their friends, and we'd been raised to keep to ourselves."

"How lonely," Aimee says. She doesn't dwell on it. Instead, she does a double take at the sight of a young couple, arm in arm, approaching a nearby table.

"You know them?" I ask. The guy looks like he plays hoops. The girl is obviously wearing his letterman's jacket.

"They go to my school," Aimee says, which doesn't explain why she's hiding behind her cupcake. Or why she accidentally frosted the tip of her nose with it.

"Old boyfriend?" I ask. "Frenemy?"

Gone is the elfin warrior from last night in Nora's kitchen. Gone, too, is my street-savvy, spiritual guide. "Enrique?" she whispers. "Ancient history."

The guy glances over, and Aimee gives him a shy wave.

Enrique smirks and smacks his girlfriend on the rump.

It bothers me more than it should, especially after Aimee's declaration that we can't be friends. "Hey, Aimee . . ." I begin.

She absently licks her lips. "Hmm?"

I take it as an invitation, lean across the table, and kiss her full on the mouth. It's a sugary kiss — one that lingers. She tastes like mango passion and surprise.

"Thanks," I say. I give her a quick peck on the nose, and that's it for the smeared icing. When I settle back down, Enrique's girl is staring at us. At me, actually.

Pre-kiss me might've met her inviting gaze. Post-kiss me doesn't bother. Meanwhile, Enrique looks like he wants to beat me into the ground.

Tough luck, loser.

"You didn't have to do that," Aimee whispers, though it's clear she didn't mind. "Enrique doesn't matter anymore." Before I can follow up on that, she begins trying to sell me on the idea of including Clyde in our search for my sister.

"He's already decided Ruby's guilty," I remind her, practically inhaling my chocolate cupcake.

"For now, you two can agree to disagree," Aimee tells

me. "If you're right that your sister is innocent, then there's nothing to worry about."

"Unless Clyde shoots first and asks questions later," I reply.

Aimee wipes icing from her mouth. "Clyde? He's more likely to sprout a tail or vamoose to Mexico. He talks big, but at the first sign of danger, he usually bails or plays dead, except . . ."

"Except what?" I ask.

A couple of sweaty, burly guys wearing orange construction vests take the table next to us. They grin, toast us with their cupcakes, and then tune their boom box to NPR.

Aimee lowers her voice. If I wasn't a shifter, I couldn't have heard her.

"A few months ago, Clyde and I went with some friends on this monsterpalooza of a road trip. We ended up in this little German town in Michigan and—"

"Monsterpalooza?" Fine, I can play. "Like Frankenstein's monster? The Loch Ness monster? Bigfoot?"

She bites one of her fingernails, chipping the green polish. "Like Count Dracula, for example. Dracula Prime, the original."

"You sure you don't mean Count Chocula?" I ask. I'm willing to accept that Aimee and other rational people believe in vampires. Grams believed in vampires—not that she was rational. But *Dracula* is pushing it. Life is not a Bela Lugosi movie.

111

"Just listen," Aimee replies. "In the middle of this torrential storm, the Count grabs me by the throat on Main Street, and Clyde — Clyde — comes roaring after us."

I'm not hungry anymore. "You're saying the Possum saved your life?"

"He tried, and almost died in the process. It took a healing spell that blew the roof off a house to wake him from the coma he was in." Aimee points to the tattooed crosses around her neck. "But technically, this saved my life."

I gauge her body language, heart rate, and scent. She's sincere. Something seriously scary went down in Michigan, and even if Clyde is a pissy, gray-haired marsupial, he knows something about being a man.

CLYDE

WHEN YOSHI DROPS AIMEE OFF, I've been waiting for a while, seated on the concrete steps leading to her apartment. My new 007-worthy crutches are leaning against the stair rail. Aimee's mom already told me who she was with. "Did you forget promising to babysit the quads with me this morning?"

"I did!" Her hands fly to her face. "How'd it go?"

"When the kits wouldn't eat their organic sweet potatoes or strained grubs or anything else in the fridge, I had to break out the strawberry pudding. It came spewing back up out of their mouths and leaking all over their diapers. I had to burn my clothes." That's an exaggeration. "And shower." That's not. "I could've sent you out for that apple

113

gunk they like instead, but you didn't show or answer my texts."

"Sorry," she says, lowering her hands.

I could make it easier by asking what she did today. I don't.

"Uh," Aimee finally begins again, rocking in place. "Yoshi invited me to go with him to look for Ruby, and we have a lead." She goes on to tell me about Ruby's connection to a local music-promotion business and the conversation with Wertheimer.

"Is Ruby expected to show at the club tonight?" I ask. "Or this Paxton guy?"

Aimee sinks onto the stair beside me. "We think it's worth a shot."

I rest my elbows on my knees. "And Paxton knows where Ruby is?"

"Possibly." Aimee takes a breath. "Can you make us some fake IDs?"

Us? "I already have a fake ID."

"I don't mean you and me," she says. "I mean —"

"You and Yoshi." I watch the Cat park his enormous boat of a car. He apparently drove around the block, giving her a chance to soften me up first. I'm being handled.

I reach for the railing to stand. "You trust him? Yoshi?"

"More than I did yesterday," she replies.

I scratch my chin. "The Cat might be able to pass for twenty-one, but we can't. I've tried to buy beer at every store in the city, including the drive-thrus. A half dozen of my IDs have been confiscated."

"I have a plan," Yoshi says, jogging up to join the conversation.

Stupid Cat ears.

The fact that I sell fake IDs for thirty-five dollars a card is common knowledge at Waterloo High. So is the fact that they aren't very good and mostly rely on lazy bouncers and the use of license templates from states that send few of their own to the University of Texas (Alaska, Delaware, and Rhode Island). The key is using a real photograph of the user, which is why Yoshi suggests we do a photo shoot. After we all get makeovers.

"That's your big idea?" I ask, annoyed that Aimee invited him into my bedroom. "Sounds kind of girly."

"What's wrong with being a girl?" Aimee puts in, bouncing Clara — who is no longer pooing or spewing — on my bed. "Yoshi's right. With the right makeup and clothes, I can pass for twenty-two."

"Oh, please." I laugh. "Twenty-two?"

Gesturing at the poster of supermodel Saffron Flynn tacked to my door, Aimee informs me, "That photo was probably taken when she was fourteen years old."

From my desk chair, I glance over at the bountiful curves barely contained in a neon-blue micro bikini. "No way!"

"Way." Aimee hands me the kit so she can call one of Sanguini's hostesses. After a little small talk, she asks, "Mind if I raid your closet?"

Yoshi glances up from the glass tank that's home to my leopard gecko. He studies my face and says, "Your afternoon beard is coming in."

Shifter males — the mammals anyway — typically have to shave at least twice a day. For girls and women, it's less of an issue, though they always have thick eyebrows and my mom picks up a new bottle of Nair at the grocery store every week. "You think I should shave for tonight?" I ask.

"I think you shouldn't," Yoshi replies. "I won't either."

Right, because most teenage boys can't grow full beards, and our jaunt to the jazz club isn't about passing for human; it's about passing as adults of legal drinking age.

Even if Yoshi is making sense, I still don't like having him in my home, around my friend and family.

Cradling Clara, I get that Yoshi loves his sister. Things might get ugly — really ugly — when we catch up with Ruby, but for now, our goals are compatible. We may not have a common enemy, but we do have a common mystery.

Aimee ends the call. "Boys, I'm out of here. I'll meet you at Nora's after dinner." Holding out her palm, she adds, "Somebody give me your keys."

"Because?" I ask. I feel possessive of the Bone Chiller, but more than that, I have zero interest in riding shotgun to Yoshi.

Aimee puts her hands on her hips. "I'm not about to chase all over town by bus. Between the three of us, we have two cars. Let's split up." She's doing this on purpose so we have to get to know each other better. Handling me again.

Yoshi tosses her his keys. Now he looks like the mature one. Jerk.

Aimee catches the keys one-handed. "Skew a tad Goth, so we look like we belong together. If we're pressed, Clyde and I can fake that we're regulars at Sanguini's. Nobody needs to know that we're the kitchen help." She takes Clara from me to drop off in the nursery on the way out. "See y'all later."

After Aimee's gone, the Cat starts rummaging through my closet.

"Stop that," I say. "What do you think —?"

"I'm trying to help you," he replies. "Do you have anything that a grown man might wear? Besides jeans?"

"A lot of grown men wear T-shirts," I point out.

Yoshi yanks one from the closet and holds it up. "Not T-shirts with designs of cartoon ducks that say *Honk Your Hooters*. And I traveled light. Basically, my entire wardrobe is still in Kansas. We'll have to go shopping."

"I don't need your help," I inform him. "I'm completely capable of—"

"If you're going to pass as a legally drinking man on the town," Yoshi begins again, "you're going to have to sell it. You need to market yourself as something more than a bug-eating, pimply, prey-faced teenybopper."

"My skin isn't bad," I say, which, granted, isn't my best comeback.

"It's not so much about how you look. That's fixable. It's about how you see yourself, about confidence."

I laugh. "You're not seriously trying to go all fairy god-mother on me?"

"Honestly? I'd just as soon leave you out of it," Yoshi admits, reaching to tear my poster off the door. "But Aimee has been a big help so far, and she insists that you come with us. She claims you're her hero."

"Hero?" I say, reaching for my crutches. "Me?"

Holding open the door to All the World's a Stage, Yoshi asks, "You got a steady girl?"

Maneuvering in, I'm tempted to invent a girlfriend from school. Being that he's from Kansas (and hopefully will return there soon), it's not like he'd know the difference. But why bother? I don't care what he thinks. Much. "Nah, I'm playing the field. Why?"

"Just curious." Yoshi scans the racks stuffed with costumes and vintage clothing. He pulls out a white long-sleeved button-up shirt. "Try this with pants. The collar will cover your tattoos."

"Plenty of adults have tats," I say. "Do you have any idea what a hassle it was for me and Aimee, being underage, to

118

find a decent artist who could be bribed —"

"Sure, but the ink might draw a second glance. The idea is to slip in without anyone looking too closely. Besides, we're shooting for twenty-one plus, not eighteen plus." Yoshi glances at my high-tops. "Dress shoes — brown or black leather with laces or tassels." He gestures vaguely at my crutches. "I can carry stuff for you."

I hate that I need help. "Anything else, *Mom*?"

"Yeah," Yoshi says. "Is there a reason we're here instead of the mall?"

"Are you made of money?" I ask. "Buying new is pricey. Here, we can rent clothes for the night."

Yoshi passes the shirt to a clerk to hang in the dressing room for me. Heading toward the shoes, he says, "Smart Possum."

I try to tell myself he's not being condescending.

AIMEE

THAT EVENING, Nora answers my knock on the kitchen door. "Love the hair!"

"Don't you always?" This afternoon a salon colorist muted the green highlights into brown lowlights and pinned it up to show off my neck.

Someone has hung a blue sheet in the kitchen, and I pick up a fake Alaska ID with Yoshi's photo on it. I've always found mustaches cheesy, but his newly grown one makes me wonder whether it would tickle if I kissed him.

Of course that reminds me of the way his lips felt over cupcakes. It was a getting-to-know-you kiss, a left-me-wanting-more kiss, but what did it mean?

Was Yoshi just trying to make Enrique jealous? Or does he randomly kiss girls whenever he wants?

"All right." Nora picks up her digital camera. "Try not to look too perky. Remember, you're supposed to be at the DMV."

Setting down my bag of clothes, I pose in front of the sheet.

I can hear a football game on TV in the family room. "How're the boys?" I ask. "Have they killed each other yet?"

"They're primping." The camera flashes. "I'll get this uploaded." Nora takes a seat and gestures to the half bath off the kitchen. "You're welcome to get ready in there."

I duck in as she moves to transfer the image to Clyde's laptop, muttering about how Detective Zaleski will have a conniption fit if he finds out what she's doing. "Underage kids at a bar . . ."

Shutting the door, I wiggle into the classic black dress. The skirt is swishy, and the neckline shows off my padded curves. I accent the outfit with faux-pearl earrings, a long faux-pearl necklace (wrapped around my neck three times), and my vintage black rocker boots. They're totally broken in, and the heels are low and squared. If necessary, I can run in them. From there, I add smoky eyeliner that, coupled with my already-black nails and newly tinted hair, creates a sort of mod-vintage-me look that hopefully will fit with what the scarce online reviews hinted about the club's atmosphere.

Finally, I step into the living room, where Nora and the boys are studying my new fake ID. Clyde hands it to me. "Hot off the presses," he says.

On some level, I register that the laminate is still warm.

On another, I'm flabbergasted by the guys.

Yoshi sports a black jacket over a blue shirt and black jeans. His mustache evokes swashbuckler, sword fighter — a romantic, dashing figure from the past.

Clyde is equally well coiffed, and I'm momentarily spellbound. It must've taken a professional stylist to smooth his wiry hair, accenting its wave and making the gray gleam silver. He's grown a beard but shaved it close, creating a shadow that frames his long face, makes his cheekbones more prominent, and brings out the gold in his dark eyes.

He glares at Yoshi. "You said this look works for me."

"It does," I chime in, a second too late.

Nora reaches for the remote on the coffee table and mutes the TV. "No drinking and, sure as heck, no drinking and driving. I understand that this is something y'all feel like you have to do. But that's no excuse to pile on unnecessary risks. All three of you have my phone number. First sign of trouble, holler, and I'll be there in a flash with a three-hundred-pound werebear and a machete."

AIMEE

AT HALF PAST EIGHT P.M., the bouncer at Basement Blues flicks his eyes at us. "No."

"We've got ID," Yoshi counters.

"Hers is no good here, so you two aren't welcome, either," he decrees, gesturing toward the sidewalk. "Move along."

I trudge down the ramp. "Me?" I exclaim. "I'm the weak link?"

Clyde mutters, "I can't believe we did all that for nothing." Planting his crutches firmly ahead of him, he swings forward, again and again, toward Yoshi's car.

As we pass the nearest alley, I say, "Wait. Sanguini's isn't the only place with a rear entrance for employees and deliveries."

The boys follow me around the building and down the short concrete staircase to the propped-open back door. This time Yoshi won't have to bust our way in. Once inside, we pass a door labeled STORAGE and another labeled OFFICE.

A guy in a white cook's uniform rounds the corner and asks, "Can I help you?"

"Restrooms," I say. "We're looking for the restrooms."

He's apparently heard that before. "You took a wrong turn at the stairs. Retrace the way you came, around the corner, and then left past the red-carpeted staircase."

Seconds later, we march up the stairs and stop to stare in wonder.

I get it now. We weren't turned away because I look too young, but because I smell too human. So far as I can tell, I'm the only non-shifter in the club.

At first glance, Basement Blues is crowded, dark, and smoky, bordered on one wall by a mirrored old bar, its worn wooden floor dotted with two- and four-tops.

Then through the haze, I begin to make out the patrons more clearly.

Partially shifted wereraccoons throw back brews, tear into peanuts, and toss the shells to the floor. Next to them, a bumpy-headed I'm-not-sure-what orders an

Irish whiskey from a waitress with Deer legs. Everyone is in mid-shift and holding it steadily.

"How are they all doing that?" Yoshi asks.

From what I've been told, it's no small trick to halt and hang on to a transformation in process. Most werepeople can't manage it, and I'm guessing that being inebriated is no help. It's also risky. Faced with a shifter in mixed form, too many humans would automatically reach for a gun.

"There's a new black-market drug," Clyde replies. "It's called 'transformeaze.' Gives you amazing control in the short term, but if you get hooked, you'll never take normal shifts for granted again. You can become like a rabid animal. Some werebadger from British Columbia disemboweled his own newborn kits."

It hangs unsaid that Yoshi is unusually masterful at holding his shift.

"Hey, don't look at me!" He leads us in. "This Cat man is all natural."

I ask, "Why would anyone want to —?"

"To get off," Clyde says. "This joint is probably a cover for prostitution."

"Or maybe they just want to show their fur," Yoshi replies as we make ourselves comfortable at an available four-top. "Do you always assume the worst in people?"

"How do we find this Tornquist guy?" Clyde asks, ignoring the question.

I reach into a sequined black clutch bag, hand him the

band flyer, and gesture to the corner stage, where Fayard & the French Horns are setting up. They're Bears all right. Huge, every one of them. "They're his clients."

Right then a thick-bodied woman with a fleshy, bulbous nose and long neck passes us on her way to the bar. I whisper, "What is she?"

Yoshi flags the waitress. "Wereparaceratherium."

At my puzzled look, Clyde clarifies: "Hornless rhino." He moves the red votive candle to one side and rests his crutches against the brick wall. "How is it you can ID so many kinds of shifters, Yoshi? Aren't you from Hayseed, Kansas, or something?"

Yoshi drapes his arm around the back of my chair. "Grams entertained a lot of out-of-town company." Turning to me, he adds, "Cats, Wolves, Bears, Deer . . . those of us whose distant animal kin are still around and about our same size have a huge advantage over other types of werepeople. If we're spotted in full shift, humans tend to assume we're animals. That can still be a problem during hunting season, but—"

"I understand," I say. "The animal counterparts of some of these werepeople no longer have descendants. In a place like this, they can shift fully or even partially—"

"Without being assumed a monster," the waitress interrupts. "You snuck in a human? Boys, we don't cotton to kinky stuff here."

126

Yoshi flashes a toothy smile. "She's my sister," he explains. "Adopted."

The waitress taps a hoof and sasses, "You Cats will give teat to anything."

I can't believe she's flirting with him. She must be at least thirty.

He winks and orders a pitcher of beer and three glasses.

She makes a note. "I'll bring you a bottle of our featured microbrew, predator. Plus, water for your sister and the scavenger."

Clyde grabs her wrist, and the Deer freezes in place. Her eyes widen, like it's painful for her to keep standing there, and his lips pull back like he's ready to snarl. It's an odd way for a Deer to react to a Possum. Then again, it's an odd way for Clyde to behave, too. "A pitcher," she finally chokes out. "Three glasses. My apologies, sir."

"Hey," Yoshi interjects. "Enough, already. You've made your point."

Clyde lets go, glowering. "Listen, Mr. Metrosexual —"

"Hush," I put in. "We don't want to attract attention."

The band starts up, and we're finally quiet. I like their music. I like their black fedoras. I like the whole scene, except that I've never felt more out of place.

Yoshi, on the other hand, is clearly in his element. He rests the back of his chair against the wall. He can see the whole room that way.

As the waitress drops off our beer, I'm coughing smoke. I've never seen so many people smoking cigars and cigarettes in public — it's illegal, I think. And speaking of illegal, Clyde pours me a beer before Yoshi can. I gulp, grimacing at the taste. I should've ordered water.

After the set, Yoshi says, mostly to himself, "The band is missing their bass player and lead singer." He stands. "I'll see what I can find out. Wait for me here."

"You can't tell us what to do," Clyde calls after him.

"Stop picking at him," I say. "Your attitude isn't —"

"Chill," Clyde says. "The piano player just waved someone over. It could be Tornquist." He pushes up and grabs his crutches. "Let's find out."

YOSHI

I DIDN'T WANT Clyde and Aimee to chase after me, but I am eager to talk to Paxton. I follow a broad bull Elk in a gray suit from the stage to a corner booth that can accommodate up to ten.

Behind the circular black table, a twenty-something guy lounges with his arms stretched to either side like he owns the place. He's fit but bulky for a Cat.

I take in the backward baseball cap, the heavy gold chains, his puma-blond hair, pointed ears, and claws. It's the chains that put it over the top. He looks like a twit.

"You're Paxton Tornquist Junior?" I ask.

129

"Guilty," he replies through extended saber teeth. "Do I know you?"

"Name's Yoshi." I slide into the leather booth. "You know my sister, Ruby."

"I knew her," Paxton informs me. "Biblically, if you get my meaning."

It would've been hard to miss it. I resist the temptation to call him a liar.

"But that doesn't make me anybody special," he adds. "Ruby would do a corpse if it paid her rent — would and did. She's very open-minded, or at least very open."

Last night, I clocked the Possum for saying less. Tonight all I care about is answers. "Any idea where I can find her?" I ask.

"Yoshi, we should go," Aimee says as more Elk approach.

I'm trapped behind the table. She and Clyde were smart to stay out of the booth.

Paxton sips his vodka. "You're, what? A high-school kid? Ruby finally cuts free, and here you come, sniffing after her. Grow a pair, and get a life already."

I make a grab for him, but Paxton's already sprung to land in a tucked position on the table. Then he steps down like it's nothing, like I'm nothing.

He fingers Aimee's fake pearls. "You smell nervous and horny. Too bad you look like Tweety Bird in drag."

I'm lunging, my claws extended. Massive Elk arms restrain me from both sides.

Clyde angles himself between Paxton and Aimee. "I'm no fan of Ruby Kitahara." The petty loser bares tiny teeth. "Tell me where she is, and I'll see to it that the Armadillo King pays you the bounty on her head. You won't even have to get your paws dirty."

"Out of my way, Tiny Tim," Paxton replies, shoving Clyde into a table of drunken werebuffalo. One of the Possum's crutches catches a big male in the groin.

"You don't belong here, girlie," Paxton informs Aimee. Then he points at me. "Basement Blues is supposed to be a haven for people like us."

As he storms off, the band starts up again, and suddenly, I'm not sure if he's intrinsically an asshole, hates me because I'm Ruby's brother, or is just righteously pissed off that I brought a human into a shifters-only club.

Meanwhile, the moaning Buffalo shoves a beer-drenched Clyde into an overturned chair, but his heart isn't in it. If he and his buddies wanted to hurt the kid, they would've gored or crushed him to death by now.

Aimee rushes to help the Possum to his feet. Again. She's a lot less cavalier about Clyde when he might be hurt.

I trade a look with the Elk to either side of me. "You can let me go," I say. "And I'll walk out of here with my friends. Or you can try to kick me out and risk whatever happens next. My guess? You're paid to keep this place from getting trashed."

It's the most successful argument I've made all day.

Exiting the club, I tell Clyde, "I don't know why I let you tag along."

"Don't be such a baby," he replies. "We came here for information. I was trying to get him to trust me. But you're right: Paxton's a tool."

Finally, we agree on something. In the night air, I spot a hooded figure watching us from the roof. Then it's gone.

"Did he seem high?" Aimee asks. "His eyes were dilated."

"He was partly shifted," I say. "That can signal fear or anger or —"

"Just what the world needs," Clyde muses. "A were-predator on drugs."

I'm not convinced. "Could've been the booze."

We're almost at the car when Aimee's phone goes off. "It's for you," she says, covering the receiver. "It's Paxton."

Thinking only of my sister, I take the call.

"Sorry about that, man," Paxton says. "What went down with Ruby — it's complicated. Not something I can discuss in mixed company."

"Where'd you get this number?" I reply. "What are you talking about?"

"After close, meet me on the roof of the parking garage

132

behind the club. Don't tell anyone. Don't trust anyone. I don't want the cops or the Dillos to know we've talked."

"What did he want?" Aimee asks once I've ended the call.

Returning her phone, I say, "He warned me not to come back."

We stop by Nora's place so Clyde can shower off the stink of beer and smoke before going home. She bustles upstairs after him, promising freshly dried towels.

In the living room, Aimee pulls off her boots and joins me on the sofa. "Don't get discouraged," she says. "Paxton can't be the only person Ruby worked with at Jazz Man Bookings. We'll ask around. Once Tornquist Senior gets back to town —"

"How's Clyde?" I'm not sure why I care. Maybe it's because she cares.

"He'll be okay." Aimee casts a sidelong look up the stairs. "It's mostly his pride."

I almost tell her about Paxton's invitation to meet him later. Then I remember the way he fingered her necklace, what he dared to say. Best I leave her out of it.

Was it only last night that I considered myself too smart to meet suspicious characters in dark, secluded locations? A lot has changed in twenty-four hours.

I jog downtown from Nora's house, feeling vulnerable out in the open. But from a distance, my car is more recognizable than I am. I went running a lot back home, so I don't have to concentrate to keep my pace comfortably plausible for a human.

By the time I turn onto Fourth Street, it's almost two A.M. Music pours out of clubs as I search for Ruby in every girl I pass. My sister has her share of enemies in Austin, Texas. The question is: Does she have any friends? And if so, is Paxton one of them?

There's a sign on the elevator: OUT OF SERVICE.

I jog up one ramp then another until reaching the roof. It's roped off.

I don't see anyone, but I do detect a faint trace of smoke and incense. "Hello? Paxton?"

The bumper of the lone parked vehicle — a black Lincoln Town Car — is covered with bumper stickers. Anti-oil. Anti-war. Pro-gun?

A leather sole scrapes the concrete floor as a dart pierces my right shoulder. "Ow!" As I yank it out, another hits my thigh. "Goddamn it."

As I topple to my knees, black spots fill my vision. Dimly, I hear Paxton say, "Like I told you, it takes a Cat to catch a Cat."

Then nothing. The world goes black.

CLYDE

"YOU'RE SURE THIS IS the right parking garage?" Aimee whispers as we inch our way to the top floor, our backs along the concrete wall. We have another long ramp to go.

"Yes," I hiss, and it's mostly true. With all the background noise downtown, I only caught every third word or so of what Paxton said to Yoshi on the phone.

After changing into more casual clothes, Aimee and I told our parents that we were spending the night with Quincie and Kieren, respectively. Fortunately, neither of us had previously mentioned that said friends were vacationing up north.

"I can't believe Yoshi didn't tell us about this," Aimee says, not for the first time. She pauses, turning to face me. "Do you want to ride piggyback the rest of the way?"

"No." I really don't — talk about undignified.

"It'll go faster," she insists. "Don't be a baby. I'm not going to drop you."

I'm about to protest that I'm not a baby and that's not the issue when Travis flickers into view behind her. I don't get it. This isn't the park. Why is he here?

He's waving "No" and shaking his head.

Then I hear Yoshi's voice from the next level up, and Travis is gone by the time Aimee's head turns in that direction. Likewise from above, Paxton says something about catching a Cat, and Aimee whispers, "Yoshi's in trouble."

I'm not sure how much I care. But I can't very well let her charge up the ramp without me, and besides, Travis just showed himself somewhere other than the park for the first time. Whatever's going down, it's huge.

I hop onto Aimee's back, she wraps her arms around my knees, and as she motors up the ramp, I hold the crutches so they don't drag.

On the rooftop, Yoshi is sprawled on the cement. He's unconscious, and Paxton is wrapping his long legs in heavy chains. There's a gun lying next to them.

Aimee stumbles, and for the third time in two days, I hit the ground hard. So much for stealth — if Paxton didn't hear us coming, he certainly knows we're here now.

Aimee pushes to her hands and knees, then hesitates, caught between her fight and flight instincts. She asks me, "You okay?"

"Paxton!" calls a woman's voice. "Do something."

As he reaches for the gun, I crawl a few inches with my bent arms to grab one of my secret-agent crutches. I'm raising it to fire at Paxton when a dart hits the side of my neck. My field of vision goes wavy, and it's all I can do to whisper Aimee's name.

When I wake up, I'm nauseated and achy, but I've become used to pain. I risk opening my eyes against the midday sun and discover that I've been transported to a large out-door cage. The bars along the sides are thick, the floor and ceiling solid metal. I taste heavy, clean air, and note that the plant life is lush and tropical.

Inhaling, I detect an unfamiliar, Cat-like scent. "Where . . . ?" I whisper. "Aimee?"

I sit up to greet the golden gaze of the half-naked were-lion held prisoner in the cage beside mine. Clearing my throat, I ask, "Who're you?"

She yawns — gorgeous, sweaty, and unimpressed.

AIMEE

"WHERE AM I?" I demand, chasing Sandra down a slightly uneven lava-stone staircase. "What is this place? How long was I out? What are you doing here?"

Moments earlier, I woke up, shivering, dressed in a lime-colored sundress with white socks, sneakers, and sporting a locked ankle cuff in what looks like staff housing at a resort hotel. My own clothes and boots were left in a neatly folded stack on the dresser. I found my wallet (and cash) in the pockets, but no phone.

The woman I know as Enlightenment Alley's store manager intercepted me, running out the door. "This is a small, privately owned tropical island in the Pacific," she replies. "And it's only Monday."

I'm not in Texas. I'm not even in North America. I catch the stair rail, coming around a wide corner, slipping a bit on the polished bamboo floor. "Like Hawaii?"

Bustling down the hall, Sandra says, "In the sense that it's a tropical island in the Pacific, yes. In every other sense, not at all. This isn't the United States. You aren't a citizen here. You have no rights."

I follow her into a conference room filled with clean-cut young adults dressed like I am — the women in lime-colored sundresses with white piping along the pockets, the men in matching short-sleeved button-up shirts and white pants. They all have dyed white hair, too, like Sandra's. Pulling one of my own curls forward, I realize mine matches. Someone must've done it when I was unconscious.

I scan the group, searching for Clyde and Yoshi. "Where are my friends?"

Sandra clasps her hands behind her back. "The crippled Possum has been safely deposited in an outdoor enclosure. The Cat prowls wild in the jungle, as befitting the nature of the beast he is. All of you have a purpose in service to *Homo deific*."

From my time with shifters, I've grown used to passing references to different species. Roughly translating, I ask, "God people?"

Sandra raises her chin. "They have very high self-esteem."

"What is my purpose here?" I lift my ankle, indicating the cuff. "What's that?"

"Relax. It's simply to ensure you stay in the lodge during your transitional period," she says. "Try to remove the anklet or leave this building, and you'll lose the leg."

My hand rests protectively on my thigh. "Was that supposed to be reassuring?"

Sandra goes on as if it's no big deal. "Initially, you'll likely be assigned a housekeeping task or two here in the main building. Perhaps, in time, you will become a valued team member, like me, or, if necessary, offered as a sacrifice to a future guest with a craving to satisfy."

"Craving as in sex or food?" I want to know.

"Blood, most likely," Sandra replies, "but, really, any of the above."

How flexible. "Why didn't you just kill me? Why bring me here at all?"

"I could use the company," she admits. "You were such a polite shopper at Enlightenment Alley. Your mother raised you right."

It's then that an almost seven-foot-tall, furry biped creature wearing round, wire-framed glasses proceeds from behind lime-colored curtains to the lectern.

It positions itself in the skylight glow and raises its hairy white arms as if calling an orchestra to attention. It says something in Spanish, and the group mimics it back to him. Then, in English, it looks at me and intones,

"Every day in every way, you will contribute to the profit margin of *Homo deific*."

Sandra nudges me, and I realize that I've been appropriated as the corporate handmaiden of a fugly love child of a Wookiee and the Abominable Snowman.

Given that I'm not inclined to test my anklet, for now I have no choice but to play along. Squaring my shoulders, I declare, "Every day in every way, I will contribute to the profit margin of *Homo deific*."

"Good," the snowman grunts. "Sandra, find the new one a purpose."

There's that word again: purpose. Sex, food, blood — what was my other option? House servant. I whisper, "I have restaurant experience."

YOSHI

THE MOIST, WARM AIR is briny, scented by seaweed. I squint through heavy eyelids, gazing for the first time at an ocean. I take in the white-crested waves, the epic blue.

This is no time to lose myself in wonder — frantic hoofbeats close in from the nearby jungle. Groggy, I can't begin to defend myself against whatever it might be. Alone on the beach, I've got nowhere to hide. If I choose the sea, will it dive in after me?

I force myself to stand, shaky, as a feral hog bursts around an immense fern and onto the pale sand. It's no Wilbur, and at over two hundred pounds of muscle, it's barreling my way. I take an uncertain step, and, trying to project predator, plant my legs more firmly. It's no use. I tumble, expecting to be gored.

Then an immense bear — no, a werebear — roars out of the greenbelt, giving chase. The hog gallops by. I don't matter. I'm not the thing that's trying to kill it right now.

Seconds later, the Bear overtakes the grunting hog with enormous claws. Sand sprays up, and a cracking sound rises from the swine's thick neck. It's a merciful kill.

I leverage myself on one elbow as the Bear bounds, splashing, into the sea. It disappears for a moment as if dancing in the waves. Beyond the uneven shoreline, dorsal fins veer in his direction. "Hey!" I shout. "Get out of there!"

Twice, maybe three times, I catch a glimpse of the Bear's head.

"Shark!" I add, because so what if I'm wrong and they're dolphins or it's too shallow for them to come close in. Better safe. "Please! You're a land mammal."

I'm about to yell again when he surfaces, naked in human form.

Most werepeople don't feel awkward about nudity. Fully shifting with clothes on is painful and trashes the outfit. It makes sense to start out in the buff, and you end up that way regardless. But I don't know this guy at all, so I keep my gaze well above his waist.

"What're you hollering about?" he asks.

"Uh . . ." I guess the fins are still fairly far out. "Shark?" I saw *Jaws* on TV at an impressionable age.

He uses his hand like a visor to scan the horizon. "Not exactly," the Bear calls, lumbering toward his prey. "My name's Luis. I'm one of the good guys. You?"

I push up. "Yoshi." Checking my pockets, I say, "They took my comb."

He laughs. "And your phone, if you had one. Can I borrow your T-shirt?"

I stagger across the hot sand to meet him.

Luis adds, "I need to tie off the hog's leg wound so it doesn't trail blood."

He must've almost caught it with his claws. Peeling off my sweaty shirt, I ask, "Who are you, Luis?"

"The biggest badass bass player west of I-35 and south of Seattle." He rips off my sleeves and bends to wrap the leg. "How'd you end up here?"

I don't mention Ruby by name or that she's a murder suspect, but I hit the highlights of my story up to falling for Paxton's trap at the garage. "Next thing I knew—"

"You woke up on the beach," Luis says. "That's how it usually goes. The lead-up details are different from shifter to shifter, but they usually involve the club somehow and Paxton typically dumps newbies here or at the farthest end of the island from their compound." Luis lifts the hog to rest across his linebacker-size shoulders. "Welcome to the South Pacific. At least that's where I think we are."

"Looks like paradise," I say, and it does. The sand is

radiant, the jungle an enchanting green, the ocean frothy and inviting . . . except for the fins.

He laughs. "What's your idea of paradise?"

I give it a moment's thought. "Somewhere that nobody's trying to shoot me."

"Well," the Bear replies, "you're going to hate it here. Feeling up for a hike?"

"Sure." My head is clearer now. I pull my now-sleeveless shirt back on.

"This is a small, private island." Luis points up at sheer rock cliffs in the distance. "That mountain, volcano, whatever, is the far border or at least cuts off this hunk of land from whatever might be on the other side."

"Private as in privately owned?" I ask, remembering that Paxton's from money.

"Right," Luis says, adjusting the hog. "They've stocked this island with a variety of shifters — like you and me — who're considered hard kills. Desirable trophies."

As we plunge into the jungle, I extend my claws to hack through tropical leaves and vines. "You mean someone's *hunting* us?"

"Not at the moment." Luis sets down the hog and pulls on tattered cutoffs that he left behind on a boulder, along with a canteen and binoculars. He secures the canteen to one of his belt loops and tosses the binoculars to me. "Keep your eyes open. Ears, too."

I frown. "You're saying Paxton —"

"He's the least of your worries now," Luis informs me. "It's better if I show you."

I'm already soaking wet from the humidity.

We keep hiking, startling a goat on the way. Luis explains that there apparently have been countless efforts to settle this island, sailors bringing with them pigs, goats, rats . . . what for us is easy prey. "The white-tailed deer is good eating. Stay away from the monkeys. They're cute, but they steal and bite."

"What about snakes?" I ask. "Scorpions?"

"Yep."

"Are they poisonous?"

He gives me a look. "If one bites you, we'll find out."

"What about big predators?" I add. "Jaguars or . . . ?" I'm not sure what exactly, but I have a vague memory of watching giant poisonous lizards on the Discovery Channel.

"Not that we've seen," Luis replies. "At least not in recent memory."

Maybe there aren't any, which is why smaller animals are so plentiful — no alpha predator — or maybe they were hunted to extinction. At least there's food.

Fresh water, too, I discover as we hike up a stream.

"Shortcut," Luis says. "Watch your step."

The rocks are sharp, slippery. I cut my ankle twice. But

146

it's quicker going this way, and the waterfall is breath-taking. After a while, we're back on solid land.

At the base of a thirty-some-foot-high ridge, Luis sets the hog down. I scale up after him, reaching the top first.

"Lay of the land," he announces, panting. "Look there."

I raise the binoculars. Beyond the jungle is a rustic three-story building. The area just ahead of it has been partially cleared and artfully landscaped. Escape can't be that easy. Plus it's an awful big building for just Paxton. "The bad guys?"

"Yep." Luis points out to sea.

"A boat!" I exclaim. A small yacht, I think.

"One of theirs," he tells me. "The only way to the dock is through the main building, and the rat bastards have set up a high-frequency barrier to keep us out."

I think about it. "Like one of those invisible dog fences?"

"Only it makes your brain bleed out your ears. It runs from the natural rock wall far into the ocean," Luis explains. "We've tested it. Didn't go well."

I consider how I got here. "Copters?"

"They come and go," Luis says. "So far as we can tell, they only linger long enough to refuel. Not that I know how to fly a helicopter. Do you?"

"Not so much," I admit. "Who are 'they' anyway? Besides Paxton."

"Check out the top of that sheer cliff above the main property," Luis suggests.

I do and, with a gasp, lose my footing. Only the Bear's reflexes save me from tumbling down and breaking my neck.

Those armed guards can't be albino wereapes. There's no such thing as wereapes of any fur color. They're not polar werebears. The body type is all wrong. Besides, they have the dome-shaped heads of modern humans.

"There's a scientific explanation," Luis puts in. "An evolutionary chart and a whole lot of big words to explain it. But I just think of them as goddamned greedy yetis."

CLYDE

THE HOUR I JUST WASTED trying to tear apart this cage suc-
ceeded only in making me as sore as I've been since first
coming out of the coma last September. The thing making
me really crazy, though, is that my captors left my electro-
charged crutches propped just out of reach against the
trunk of a nearby palm tree. No matter how hard I strain,
my covert super weapons are resting a tantalizing six
inches beyond my fingertips.

Lacking a better option, I stretch out on a rope hammock. There's also a hanging water bottle and a pile of
straw in the corner that I assume is supposed to be my
toilet. I refuse to go until after my unspeakably sexy fellow
prisoner falls asleep.

She may think she's proving something, giving me the silent treatment. But I've been rejected by tons of girls. I don't give up that easily. It's time to give conversation another shot. "Do they feed us here, or have we been left to starve?" I doubt it's the latter. She looks awfully healthy to me.

A honeyed voice replies, "Either Paxton will come or one of their pet humans. It may take a day or two."

Is that what happened to Aimee? Is she being kept as a pet? Not that I'm hugely uncomfortable at the moment, with my ankles crossed and my hands behind my head. "You finally decided to talk to me?"

"I'm bored. You're here." My neighbor stretches her arms above her head. "I'm Noelle, by the way."

"Clyde," I reply. "I've never met a Lion before."

"Lioness," she corrects me.

And despite my winning personality, she keeps to herself for the rest of the afternoon.

Unlike the ravishing Noelle, I can't sleep. (Lions, like all Cats, are known for their love of napping.) I grip the cage bars, stare out at the elusive crutches. All of this is Yoshi's fault. I wouldn't be in this mess if that Cat —

"Stewing about Yoshi is not going to help," Travis's voice scolds. "And no, I'm not psychic. I just know you that well."

Chilled, I wobble back toward the center of the cage.

"I . . . How? This isn't the neighborhood park . . . and you were in that garage downtown, too."

"The park was never a haunted place," Travis begins, taking shape. "You're a haunted person, or wereperson, if you want to get technical about it. I have some leeway to float around the astral plane, but for the most part, you're my worldly anchor."

"You watch me all the time?" I exclaim. "Like some kind of angel?"

"Nah." He wrinkles his nose. "I can only move in a mile or so radius around—"

"Aimee!" I instinctively try to grab him by the shoulders. As my hands slide through his image, I say, "I think she's in the lodge. Go check on her. Tell her—"

"I can't tell her anything," Travis insists. "In exchange for permission to linger on earth, I promised an archangel that I'd restrict my haunting to you."

AIMEE

LATER, SANDRA TOURS ME around the lodge like she's a corporate recruiter. "This is where the interns gather for meals," she says.

From what I understand, she's the sole team member and every other human of our kind is a student intern, apparently now including me. I glance around the room. The furniture is black rattan, and the space is decorated with framed scrimshaw and an antique globe.

Like the uniforms, the long curtains are lime green with white trim. So are the chair cushions, rug, tablecloth. . . . A massive watercolor portrait of a snowman wearing wire-framed glasses is framed in black rattan with a lime-green mat.

How quaint and lovely, and never mind that I've been kidnapped and separated from my friends! Not that freaking out will help. I can do this. I'll ask the right questions and somehow Nancy Drew my way to a workable plan.

"Does anyone besides you and me speak English?" I ask, having learned after the snowman motivational business meeting that she's bilingual, English-Spanish. The other interns are all traditional college-age and from Central or South America.

"The deific leadership does," Sandra informs me. "That and Spanish for business purposes. They've traditionally focused on the North American market. This is a new territory for them. In any case, they're pleased to have another native English speaker on the island. So much of their business is conducted on the phone. They practice all the time, but it's hard for them to feign a passably human accent."

I never thought of my entire species as having an accent, but the snowman who spoke at the lectern did have a guttural voice. It might have had something to do with his physiology. Following her down the wide, carpeted hall, I ask, "What is this place? What do you do here, besides —?"

"I am Boreal's emissary for face-to-face dealings with the human world related to this enterprise. Only so much can be done long-distance, even in this day and age." Sandra lingers at a picture window to show me the view of the endless ocean below. "The interns are in training to do the same for his new and planned ventures throughout this region of the world."

"Why would they —?"

"Money, of course." Sandra rests her hand on my shoulder. "He finances their higher education, offers full medical coverage — including dental — from top-notch doctors, and generously supplements their families' income back home.

"After winter break, most will return to their respective colleges to study finance, accounting, marketing, business, and the like. Those who maintain the property on a day-to-day basis — the maids and groundskeepers and handymen — are enrolled in independent studies or taking a semester off."

I wish she would stop touching me.

Sandra goes on, "Your mother has been struggling financially since the divorce, hasn't she? You know, my father abandoned my family when I was about your age." She reaches into her pocket and pulls out a photo of a thirty-some-years-younger version of herself, standing in front of a beat-up trailer home with four younger freckled kids and a woman I assume is her mother. "Today, they're living large in a gated community in Palm Beach. They think they won the Florida State Lottery. I got to go to college at MIT, went on to receive my MBA at Georgetown, make seven figures a year, and occasionally have free time to indulge my passion for community theater."

I shiver under the air-conditioner duct. "I'm not all that academic."

Stashing the photo away, Sandra nudges me toward what looks like a sundries shop. I wander in, studying the rows of toothbrushes and paste, shoelaces and sewing kits, Band-Aids, maxi pads, chamomile drops, cotton swabs, invisible tape. . . .

"We couldn't leave you in Austin," she replies. "You already knew too much, and I personally would never harm a fellow mono-form human being."

If Sandra's the reason I'm alive, I should probably keep courting her favor. "I've always loved visiting Enlightenment Alley. Ever since I was little, I thought it was magic."

"How quaint." She hands me a plastic bag from a stack on the unoccupied counter, and I realize I'm supposed to be loading up. Sandra adds, "I was sent to infiltrate the store as an in to Tornquist Senior's businesses. He built much of his fortune catering to his fellow werebeasts. A lot of shifters are Enlightenment Alley regulars. Perhaps it's the influence of their animal forms, but they tend to be environmentalists, and of course the Wolves are huge readers. There are currently six *Canis dirus sapiens* in our Women Who Run as Wolves Book Club, which meets on the second Thursday of every month."

I can forget appealing to Sandra's social conscience. Scanning the shelves, I see that there are no razors, no metal nail clippers. I remember knives being pre-set in the breakfast room. Maybe I'm allowed sharp objects only in supervised company.

"Between us," Sandra continues, "I'm lonely here. I'm not of the deific, and the interns come and go. At first, you'll be expected to help with menial chores, but I have high hopes of fast-tracking you to assist me when the occasion arises. Say, when I'm back in Austin or when clients are in residence on the island for a hunt."

Joy. I'm her new protégé. Or maybe she's keeping a close eye on me until she's sure I can be trusted, in which case — wait. "Hunt?" I repeat, tightening my grip on a roll of Lifesavers candy. "What hunt?"

That evening, Cameron, the cook, lifts one of the glass mugs I polished and holds it to the overhead light. "Flawless. You really did work in a pro kitchen."

"Five stars from *Tejano Food Life*," I reply, covertly studying his horns. I've seen plenty of faux devils dining at Sanguini's, but Cameron is the first real demon I've ever met. He has a spiked red tail sticking out of a hole in the back of his jeans.

Not my first choice for companionship, but he's at least distracting me from obsessing over the upcoming hunt. I can't believe they even call it that, a hunt, as opposed to, say, a psycho killing spree. Plus I can't really talk to the interns. I think a couple of them can understand some of what I'm saying, even if they don't know enough English to reply. One girl even proudly showed me her semester-one English textbook. But it's hard to communicate anything meaningful, and I despise them for being here willingly . . . assuming they are here willingly. I'm honestly not sure about that, either.

Cameron moves to the stove and stirs the yak-leek soup. "Taste test?"

I sip from the ladle. "Do you have kosher salt?"

He pivots to the spice cabinet. "I have sea salt."

Cameron oddly reminds me of that Westlake shrink my parents took me to after they broke the news that they were getting a divorce. Easy to talk to, charming even, but like it's somehow costing you more than you can afford. He smells splendid, though, like cotton candy and peppermint.

While he tinkers with the first course, I load the chilled mugs onto a round tray and deliver them to the candlelit table in the formal dining room.

Right then, ten of the so-called deific file in, chatting about the market price for gold versus the strength of the U.S. dollar and the possible influence of the euro on both.

I grab the chilled pitcher of pale lager and weave around them, ducking in again and again to fill mugs. I've already positioned a glass of ice water at every place setting. For the most part, they consider me beneath their notice, which is a relief. I scan the table once more, mentally confirming that — yes — I left four more pitchers so

157

they can pour their own refills. (Cameron assured me that trying to keep up with their drinking on a mug-by-mug basis is a lost cause.)

The one lady of the house gets a glass of V8 served with a green straw and garnished with green olives. She's apparently in a family way.

Strolling out, I can't resist sneaking a closer look. They stand upright and walk with a humanlike gait, but their arms are slightly longer and their jaws are noticeably bigger than those of *Homo sapiens*. From what I understand, they originally hail from some remote wintry homeland but have been steadily infiltrating the rest of the globe since the invention of air-conditioning, which is why it's so blasted cold indoors.

"Tell me, Cameron," I begin, back in the kitchen. "What's a chipper culinary fiend like you doing playing chef to a pack of overgrown fuzz balls?"

He fills soup bowls and places them on my tray. "I wouldn't underestimate them, kiddo. Those fuzz balls have been around since before the Neanderthals debuted on the scene. They outlived them and *Homo erectus* and the hobbits."

"So you're firmly on board?" I ask. "You live to contribute 'every day and every way' to their profit margin?"

Cameron garnishes each bowl with chives. "Hardly. I'm a demon. De-mon. I bow only to the Prince of Darkness himself." And yet he reaches for the pepper grinder.

"Any reason they decided to open up shop on a *tropical* island? I mean, it's clear the snowmen aren't here for the sunshine."

Cameron gives me a look like I'm asking a few too many questions, but he doesn't care enough to mind. "They tried a couple of hunts in the Arctic, but they ran into weather delays, a few clients froze to death, and there was an influx of mainstream media in the region when some whales got stuck in the ice. Here, all they've got to worry about is the occasional hurricane, which is what those huge shutters are for." He chuckles. "Fuzz balls, snowmen . . . Just don't call them cryptids. They find any implied association with Bigfoot undignified."

"It must be hard, living completely undetected as a species." Not that, under the circumstances, I feel sorry for them. "But I guess werepeople did it for centuries."

As I hoist the tray over my shoulder, Cameron adds, "You'd be surprised by how much is out there in the world, in the underworld, even in us, waiting for its moment."

Aren't we the demonic fortune cookie? Before I can think more about it, there's shouting from the dining room.

"Scoot!" Cameron urges. "I'll load up another tray." He holds the door open, whispering, "Serve the leaders first. Boreal, the one wearing spectacles? He's the head male. His mate, Crystal, is opposite him. Frore, at Boreal's right, with the braids hanging in his eyes, is the second-in-command."

The rest are guards who watch over the grounds. Another shift has taken their place.

As I begin the dinner service, Frore says, "Lion genes should be dominant."

Boreal tosses his spoon across the room. "Enough! I will not be swayed."

Whatever that's about . . . It's only after the room falls quiet that I notice I've spilled soup on Crystal's white fur. She dips her napkin into her ice water and dabs at it.

Should I apologize? Am I allowed to speak at all?

"Are you quite all right, dear?" Boreal asks.

"Yes, not to worry," she replies, her manners dainty. "This one is new. It's probably still in shock. Let's give it a day or two to settle in."

I exhale and deliver Frore's soup, wishing I'd lobbied for a lower-profile job.

"I don't know how you can tell them apart," Frore replies. "They're all so ugly."

"That one is a female," Boreal says. "You can tell from its tiny breast buds."

He did *not* just say that. Then again, I can't tell any of them apart, except for Boreal because of his specs, Frore because of his braids, and Crystal, who's smaller than the males, rounded from the pregnancy, and whose fur hangs in fuzzy spiral curls, apparently due to a catastrophic home perm. I drop off the last bowl to a guard.

"They're such bald creatures," Crystal muses. "Like hairless house cats."

"Hairless house cats," Frore echoes with a shudder.

Ankle cuff or no, I've got to find Clyde and Yoshi and get the hell out of here. The lodge is off the grid. No Internet, no phone service.

No matter. I just have to keep up this chatty, disarmingly cute act, figure out what's going on, and connive a way off of this island for me, the boys, and whoever else needs saving. And then I'm going to adopt a hairless house cat and treat it like royalty.

CLYDE

PAXTON SHOWS UP, pushing a metal food cart, and shoves a plate of milky oats through a slot in the cage bars. He's ditched the heavy gold-chain necklaces from the club, revealing ugly, deep scars around his collarbone.

"Where's Aimee?" I demand. Travis hasn't reported in yet, and I don't know if that's because he couldn't find her or because he's lost track of time mooning over her. Back when he was alive, he used to do that a lot.

"Your girl? Unless she's managed to piss off the deific, which can be fatal, she's their newest intern. Robotic, corporate, pedestrian fashion — tragic, let me tell you."

Noelle finally filled me in on our kidnappers. "You're one to talk," I counter, "selling out your fellow shifters to a bunch of overgrown arctic asshats."

"Go play dead," Paxton replies. "You know why you're still alive? You're nothing but a companion animal for Noelle. Like when horse breeders let the old mares out to pasture with their prize champions. Piss me off, and it's the glue factory for you."

I could've lived without him saying that in front of the Lioness.

Carrying a platter of meat, piled high, he approaches the slot in her cage.

Noelle saunters over as if to accept the meal and, as he leans in, lashes out through the bars with extended claws.

Paxton jerks back and flashes his teeth. "Naughty kitty! I'd let you starve, if this gig weren't so damn profitable."

Spotting my crutches against the nearby tree, he sets the plate on the three connected bars at the top of one and moves to try to feed her again.

"Grab it!" I yell once the underarm cushion is within her reach. "The crutch!"

"What?" Noelle is already holding the platter of food. "What're you —?"

With a sneer, Paxton tosses the crutch so it lands on the metal roof of my cage. He doesn't know why I want it so badly. He's just getting off on torturing me.

163

Returning his attention to Noelle, Paxton adds, "Yak ribs fit for a queen."

She sniffs her food and retreats toward her hammock, and it's then that I notice her limp. "I'm not interested in your favors," Noelle says.

She's not just talking about the menu.

"You sure?" he asks. "Clients keep telling the deific that they want to bag a head with a mane — makes for a nice trophy over the fireplace mantel."

Noelle tears off a hunk of meat. "What would you know about having a mane?"

Paxton strikes a pose that I've seen Yoshi work to great success, but Paxton can't quite pull it off. "If they can't locate a male Lion soon, the deific might take a chance on breeding you with another type of Cat."

Noelle shakes her head. "Remember what happened last time you got too close?"

She's the one who'd marked Paxton. Is that how she injured her foot?

"You can only hold out so long." He runs a suggestive hand down his chest. "You and I used to play together just fine, and we kitties have our appetites."

Ew. Whatever was between Noelle and Paxton, it ended badly.

YOSHI

LUIS AND I SHOWERED and refilled the canteen at the waterfall. We tied the hog's front and back hooves, respectively, together with vines, slipped a straight branch beneath them, and are hauling it (Luis in front, me behind him) on our shoulders. It's not that heavy, but he's taller than me, and I keep tripping on the undergrowth.

I've been able to smell campfire smoke for a while.

"Almost there," Luis says. "They're first-rate folks — you'll see."

Between birdcalls, I catch snatches of conversation on the wind. At least one of the voices is feminine. Moments later, through the greenery, I make out a few figures — two slender, one burly and bulky. I catch the scent of berry, fish, Wolf, more Bear.

"*Hola*, fellow castaways," Luis announces. "This is my man Yoshi."

As we toss the hog into a fire pit, Luis introduces Mei, James, and Brenek. They look wired but healthy, rested and well fed. I haven't forgotten what Luis told me about the yeti-hosted "big game" hunts, but we're a Cat, two werewolves, and two werebears. I can hardly think of a more impressive combination of land werepredators. What on earth would be stupid enough to come after us?

"Yoshi Kitahara?" Brenek repeats, extending an enormous hand. He's about my age, maybe a little younger, with a midwestern accent.

I hesitate before shaking. "Do I know you?"

"I work with your sister," he says. "Or at least I used to."

It takes me a minute to process. "You know Ruby? I've been looking —"

"Eat first," Mei insists, glancing at her digital watch. "Talk later. The humidity zaps your strength. Food will help."

When I open my mouth to protest, Brenek adds, "She's right. Enjoy. Catch your breath. Then you can join me on first night watch. If you're not too worn out, that is."

Ah. He wants to speak with me privately. Fine, I've waited this long.

Making small talk, I learn that the werewolves are newlyweds, New Yorkers, and second-semester grad students at UT. She's in botany. He's in engineering.

Wolves have a reputation for being book smart and hyper-competent. It can be annoying, but these two seem all right. Paxton captured them biking along the lakefront. They'd been planning to fly out for a five-day, six-night honeymoon in Orlando that evening. They're still kicking themselves for not taking an earlier plane.

I repeat the version of my story that I told Luis. The conversation oddly reminds me of Kansas, where the first question old folks often ask is "How'd you get here?"

"Fresh catch of the day," Mei announces, presenting me with a two-foot-long roasted fish on a large palm leaf. "It'll take a while to cook the hog."

Suddenly ravenous, I eat with my fingers, periodically blowing on them to cool them off. The fish tastes like tuna-y heaven. James cracks open a coconut for me, too.

After a few bites, I say, "I appreciate the hot meal, but don't the campfires give away our location?"

"It won't matter with the hunters," Luis explains. "But a plane might spot the smoke, and it keeps the bugs away. There are mosquitoes here the size of ponies."

I've noticed. "What's with the berry body paint? The

holy symbols?" I can't decipher the Chinese characters on Mei and James, but the newly inked crosses on Brenek's neck, wrists, and pulse points remind me of Clyde and Aimee's neck tattoos.

"The hunters are usually proficient in demonic magic," Luis explains. "These markings may help protect us against certain spells."

"And some vampires," Brenek puts in. "It varies from vamp to vamp. But the wards are useless against guns, which can kill you just as dead and from a distance."

I dip my fingers into the berry mix and paint COEXIST in religious symbols down my arms — just in case. I'm not a trained fighter. Ruby is so tenderhearted that she wouldn't even let me chase squirrels.

Only Luis has survived a previous hunt. That makes him the expert.

"We know what doesn't work." He makes himself comfortable by the fire. "Infighting or taking an every-shifter-for-himself attitude. Our best chance of survival is working together."

Clearly, he's the alpha. That's fine. I don't want the job, and it's less terrifying knowing that these fellow werepredators have pledged to back me up.

Posturing aside, most Cats aren't all that independent. I didn't make it twenty-four hours on my own in Austin before Nora took me in.

"Understood," I say as Luis and James begin striking

rocks together to make hand axes and knives. "You can count on me."

While we're still within hearing range of the other shifters, Brenek explains that hunts are traditionally announced by a horn blasting from the lodge side of the island.

"How do we know a warning is standard procedure?" I ask. "Luis has only been in one hunt, right?" I'm doing better, navigating the dense jungle, letting my animal instincts take charge and flow.

"One of the shifters that Luis met, a pygmy were-elephant, had made it through three previous rounds," Brenek explained. "She told him."

It goes without saying that she died last time out. "Should we be doing a better job of hiding?" I ask again. "Our campsite isn't camouflaged, and with the smoke—"

"Wouldn't matter," he replies, echoing Luis. "The hunters typically use locator spells or—"

"Then why don't they just kill us with a snap of their fingers and be done with it?" As soon as the words are out, I'm embarrassed. I expect Brenek to reassure me or yell at me to stop being such a wimp.

"They might," he says instead, and then he changes the subject to recent college and pro sports, claiming the Chicago Bears football team is actually named after local werebears. It's entertaining, but total BS—I think.

It gets dark fast, daylight to almost pitch-black in

maybe half an hour. Fortunately, Cats see well in low light. I block a palm leaf from smacking my face.

Unable to wait any longer, I finally ask, "Did you work with Ruby at Sanguini's or the music-promotion company?" Before Brenek can answer, I figure out where I saw him before. "It was you! You were at her place with the priest."

"Guilty," he says, climbing the overlook rock. "I might as well admit that I recognized your scent from her apartment." He glances over his shoulder. "Ruby lied to you. Or at least she didn't tell you the whole truth."

Reaching for a handhold, I follow him up. "Meaning?"

"Ruby, that priest — Father Ramos — and I are operatives for an interfaith coalition," he says. "It's an international initiative, over five hundred years old."

"So you . . ." I think it over. "Hand out pamphlets and run soup kitchens?"

His laugh is joyless. "We stake vampires, hack up zombies, and trap renegade hellhounds. You know, if we're lucky and they don't kill us first."

We take a short breather on a ledge. "You're saying that you and my sister perform exorcisms on vomiting children with rotating heads?" I ask, noticing the tiny lizard who's hitched a ride up on my shoulder. I decide to leave it there.

Brenek cracks his knuckles. "We leave the heavy lifting to the clergy." As we resume climbing, he adds, "Ruby was assigned to investigate a series of missing-person cases. The leadership thought Paxton was connected, and they were right. But she kept digging and got caught up in what turned out to be separate vamp activity."

Werepeople don't tend to dabble in evil mysticism. But not everyone with a tail is a white hat. "So you moved on to other suspects, like the manager at Sanguini's."

We pull ourselves onto the summit. From a distance, a bird calls, *Tchak, tchak, tchak.* Raising the binoculars, I see torches burning outside the lodge.

"There were two sets of scumbags working out of Central Texas — vamps targeting humans, and the yetis' crew, targeting shifters. Ruby got caught in the cross fire, so to speak. Her last report was dated September twelfth. So far as we know, she's still alive."

I can only pray that's the case. "How'd she hook up with the coalition, anyway?"

"Your grandmother," Brenek replies. "She's been an operative for over thirty years."

"Get out!" I exclaim.

Wow, that explains a lot.

YOSHI

BRENEK AND I aren't back at camp five minutes before I try out one of the hammocks, made of interwoven bark and vine, secured between tree trunks. It feels good to finally relax a little. The past couple of days have pushed my endurance to the limit.

I wake around noon on Tuesday, roused by a skittering noise.

A rat scurries past the fire, raising its nose to sniff the smoke before hurrying on. Up in the trees, I spot three black monkeys with white faces sitting in a row on a branch. It's creepy, like they're studying me. I hiss. They flinch and start bouncing in place.

Something else catches my eye — a pile of seashells, each filled with multicolored blooms, bright-yellow ones shaped like trumpets and others that I recognize as orchids. Sweet. They're a gift from James to his bride.

The Wolves don't complain — none of us do — but I can't imagine this is how they planned to spend their honeymoon. They're quiet, and it's like they have an almost psychic connection. At dinner last night, Mei told me they met between seventh and eighth grade at a science camp and have never even dated anyone else. Luis has made them our official water fetchers, if only to give them some alone time.

Plus the waterfall is kind of romantic. It makes me think of Aimee, and I'm glad she's safe back in Austin. I wonder what she thinks became of me.

As I close my eyes again, I hear a cracking noise. "Who's there?"

Where did everyone go? Fishing? Hunting? I don't expect them to babysit me, but . . . I hear a footstep. A paw step? My new friends would've answered my call.

I hear another footfall against the tangled undergrowth and rush forward, leaping over a fallen tree and grabbing a vine to swing Tarzan-style.

The monkeys flee, chirping madly, as I scan the landscape below.

It's a girl! A wild child, filthy, with her short, dark hair sticking out in all directions. I drop, grabbing her by the arms. She spits and scratches and squirms.

"Stop it!" I yell as she sinks her teeth into my forearm. She's young, thirteen or fourteen, stocky and athletic, with vicious teeth. I can't ID her species by scent.

"I'm not going to hurt you," I assure her. It sounds ridiculous in light of the blood streaming down my arm. "I'm Yoshi. What's your name?"

Apparently deciding she can't gnaw through me to freedom, she unlocks her sharp teeth and spits at my face again. "Teghan."

Then she slams her knee into my crotch, and doubling over, I blink back stars.

The Wolves rush onto the scene, and James asks, "Who's your friend?"

By the time Luis and Brenek reappear to check the hog roast, the Wolves and I have told Teghan about the coming hunt and what we know of the yetis.

Silent, she keeps her distance, kicking a log, ready to bolt at any moment, but clearly eager to know why she's on the island and what's happening here.

Suddenly Teghan freezes in place, her eyes wide. As we were talking, we slowly spread out, and with the arrival of the Bears, she's surrounded.

"How long have you been on the island?" Luis asks.

In reply, Teghan fists her hands and clicks her teeth.

"It might help if we knew your species," I say. "What's your animal form?"

When that gets us nowhere, Mei tries next. "It's only natural that you're feeling traumatized by —"

"Shut up, bitch!" the girl snarls.

Mei merely shrugs. Most women would take offense, but she is a Wolf, after all.

"You might want to rethink your attitude," Luis says. "We're all in this together." He takes a few purposeful steps forward, and so the rest of us do the same, closing in.

Together, we're a thousand pounds of predatory impatience and intimidation.

Giving the log one last good kick, Teghan finally announces, "I am a Tasmanian weredevil. My father is a Texan, and my mother was —"

"From Tasmania?" Brenek puts in.

Narrowing her eyes, Teghan says, "Good guess."

Luis extends his hand in welcome, and after eyeing him suspiciously for a moment, Teghan shakes it and barks a laugh.

Just what we need, an unstable Tasmanian weredevil — the hands-down meanest, most depraved, and most disagreeable of all weremarsupials (though I may be biased because my arm and balls still ache).

Mei offers her a freshly boiled cloth. "Here — your cheek is bleeding."

175

The new girl's young enough that her healing ability probably isn't as strong as the rest of ours, and the last thing we need is a wound infection.

Wiping her face, Teghan glances my way. "Sorry I bit you."

It still stings. I notice she doesn't bother to apologize for kneeing me. Then again, Teghan is just a kid, and Mei was right. She's probably traumatized. "Maybe you're sorry," I reply. "But I'm not. It tells me you're a fighter."

Mei tracks down some leaves with antiseptic properties to apply to Teghan's cut and, just to be safe, my bite wound and ankle. Then she departs with the kid for the waterfall to wash up, while the Bears haul the hog out of the pit and James and I carve it with our claws.

It's a slapdash, primitive process. But we did cook the hog. We are working together. Things may have been touch and go with Teghan for a minute, but we're not going all *Lord of the Flies* on each other.

YOSHI

AFTER THE PORK FEAST, Teghan comes up with a brilliantly vicious idea, to lure the hunters into camouflaged Burmese tiger pits.

Given our animal forms, we all like to dig, and we're fantastic at it.

"I am supervising," Teghan informs us, hands on her hips like a little general.

Luis growls a low warning, asserting his alpha status.

"I am gathering brush," Teghan amends, marching off with equal enthusiasm.

"Don't go far," I call.

We've already warned the kid off fetching deadwood for the fires. You never know what's slithering in or under it. Luis is handling that job himself.

"At the last hunt," he begins, "everyone panicked at the horn. We scattered in all different directions, and they basically picked us off, one by one. This — holding our ground and luring the bad guys in — might actually work. Whatever they are . . . demons, vampires, humans, faerie . . . impaling should do them in."

"I'm not a killer," I reply, pausing to sit on my haunches.

"You have a right to defend yourself," Brenek insists, hollowing out the pit to my right. "Yourself, us, and Teghan." With a hearty grunt, he dislodges a rock. "One thing: with vamps, you've got to impale the heart or take off the head, and the older ones can turn to mist or dust, which makes that tricky."

"There may not be vampires at all," Luis puts in. "There weren't last time."

I move to help him lift out a stone. "But if so, they can be hurt."

"We'll do the best we can," James adds, hushing us as Teghan strides back into view with an armload of greenery. He glances from her to Mei, his expression pensive.

The pressure on the newlyweds is more intense than for the rest of us. It's not just about personal survival or pitching in for the team. For each of them, the person they love most is in fatal danger.

"Teghan," Mei begins as the weredevil rejoins us, "are you feeling all right? You didn't eat very much."

It's true. She picked at the pork. I don't know if I saw her actually eat any of it.

Teghan dumps the leaves onto a pile. "I'm a vegetarian. No food with a face."

Everyone else cracks up, and in fairness, it's ridiculous, coming from a young weredevil, especially under our dire circumstances.

On the other hand, Teghan can't go on like this. Mei can probably throw together a nonpoisonous salad, but Teghan needs protein to keep her strength up.

"How about clamlike things?" I grab a hand axe. "Do they have faces?"

Teghan brightens. "I don't think so."

"Come on," I say. "Maybe we can find some seaweed, too."

We've almost reached the beach when Teghan mutters, "I'm useless."

I slow down so it's easier for her to keep up. She can move fast, and she's not the slightest bit out of breath. But the jungle is dense, and I have the benefit of a Cat's agility. "You came up with the idea of the traps. That was fierce."

"I read a lot," Teghan says, scratching behind her ear. "Do you have a girlfriend?"

She's too young to have that look in her eye. Hoping

the kid will take the hint, I admit, "I've never been much of a relationship person. There was a girl. . . ." I can't help thinking of Aimee. "But at this rate, I'll never see her again."

"I'm not a relationship person, either," Teghan replies, as if she's had a world of experience. "It's nice of you to help me find something to eat. I am hungry."

I bet she's starving. "My sister, Ruby, is a vegetarian," I say. "So I understand." Not really. What's life without bacon? But I've learned to be tolerant of it.

We've almost reached the beach, and I can hardly wait. I didn't volunteer for this errand for strictly selfless reasons. The jungle's starting to make me feel claustrophobic. I'm used to the wide-open spaces of the plains.

"My big brother always made fun of my diet," Teghan informs me, scratching a bite on her forearm. "He's the favorite. My parents tell him everything first, let him do everything first. . . ." She sounds wistful. "I'm sure they're all looking for me."

"I'm sure they are." It's no time to get maudlin. "My grandmother likes my big sister better, too." Muttering, I add, "Or at least trusted her to infiltrate the evil undead while I was bored out of my mind, selling bonsai to *hakujin* in the middle of no —"

"Huh?" Teghan asks, tripping over undergrowth. "What's a *ha* —"

"Never mind," I say at the edge of the beach. "It's not important."

180

A whirring noise fills the air from above. At the sight of the helicopter, I dare to hope for rescue. Then I see the yeti leaning out, his rifle pointed in our direction.

"Teghan!" I shout, pulling the weredevil to her feet. "Back to camp! Run!"

I tear out down the sand, hoping to lead them away from her, as the copter swoops in. The propeller is deafening. No doubt the other shifters can hear it from the camp.

I've taken a dozen steps when the blow knocks me over. I roll, snared in a thick, heavy net. My hand axe is no use against it. Ditto my claws. The rope has a steel-wire core. The weredevil hesitates, half concealed in ferns. "Teghan!" I shout. "Go!"

Amid swirling sand, I glimpse her disappearing into the jungle.

AIMEE

I HAVE A SEMI-WORKABLE, kind of shaky plan, but I'll need help to pull it off.

I considered using charades to try to enlist one of the interns, but they've all signed contracts, and the penalties for breach are catastrophic. Any hint of defiance and their respective families will have no chance of financial recovery — for generations. (There's an English-language copy of the agreement in my room, still unsigned.)

Given that Cameron is literally soulless, I'm left with only one viable, not particularly good option. From a cracked-open doorway, I whisper, "*Psst!* Paxton!"

He glances around the otherwise-empty first-floor hallway. "Aimee?"

The Cat lets me yank him by the wrist into a walk-in closet stocked with linens, tissues, toilet paper, and cleaning supplies.

"I need your help," I whisper, shutting the door. Am I nervous? Yeah, I am, especially after his dominance display at the club. But I know better than to show fear.

"I don't usually do human girls," Paxton replies, reaching to stroke my cheek. "But since we're both desperate . . ."

"Shh!" I bat his hand away. "Listen, Sandra told me the snowmen are planning to get rid of you — as in permanently — after this hunt. You're too hard to control, lousy company, and they don't need such a powerful shifter to lure new ones in. They just need someone, anyone, with an 'in' to the werepeople community who can be bought." Total lie, but it sounds like the truth. I practiced it last night in front of a mirror.

As Paxton digests that, I add, "You have access to whatever sedative you used on me and my friends at that parking garage in Austin. Hand it over, and I'll see to it that we all escape the island alive." I have to make this fast. The longer we're in here, the more likely it is that one of the interns will discover us talking and report it to Sandra.

Paxton folds his arms across his chest. "Or I could steal a boat and leave you all behind. Easy peasy. No bossy, flat-chested virgins required."

I hate him. "The guard at the dock will be wary of you.

They all are." I gesture vaguely from his tight white T-shirt and blue jeans to my regulation lime-colored uniform. "To them, I'm just another intern — at most, Sandra's new English-speaking protégé."

The Cat doesn't look the slightest bit impressed.

"Think you can go it alone?" I press, taking a cautious step closer. "Best-case scenario, the snowmen will still hunt you down when you get home to the States. Or have some thug do it for them. Think, Paxton. Hunting werepeople is what they're into. They've built a thriving business around it. If we want to truly be free, we have to bring down this whole operation."

After a pause, he finally admits, "Point made. What're you suggesting?"

I flip off the light so no one notices it under the door. "Once the hunt begins, almost all of the snowmen will clear off the island, leaving the interns to babysit the place." I'd rather not risk Yoshi and the others by waiting that long, but our best chance of success will be when the snowmen's defenses are at their weakest.

I add, "Once I get the dock guard out of the way, I'll turn off the power grid, including the high-frequency barrier." I'd considered targeting the generator directly, but it's housed in an electrified cage. "Then it won't be just the two of us. We'll have the island shifters — multiple werepredators — on our side."

"Assuming the clients haven't slaughtered them all first," Paxton replies. Then as an afterthought he adds, "There's this girl, Teghan."

"What about her?" I ask, having heard a surprising tone of regret in his voice. "Since when do you care about any of them?"

"I don't," he admits. "Not for the most part. But Teghan . . . Sandra identified her at the shop and ordered me to bring her in. The deific have never featured a Tasmanian weredevil before. It gave them something new to highlight in the promotional brochure."

It's creepy, whispering with him in the dark. "You have feelings for her?"

"It's not like that," Paxton says. "She's just a kid. I don't trade in children. Besides, I've always had a soft spot for Tasmanian devils. What else do you need?"

I'm betting he's a Looney Tunes fan. I'm a Bugs Bunny girl myself. "Can you get a message to the jungle shifters and let them know the barrier is coming down? Clyde, too? He'll need help, but —"

"You don't ask for much, do you?" Paxton flips the light back on. He withdraws a narrow vial of amber liquid from the front pocket of his jeans. "Here's a dose of the drug. I've been carrying it around for self-protection." He gives me a measuring look. "*If* I can get a message to the jungle shifters, I will. If I can't, too bad — that's my best offer. But there's no guarantee they'll trust me. In fact, they probably won't."

"I'll give you code words," I reply. "Something that tells my friends I'm in on the plan." I turn my back to secure the vial under my breasts, inside my bra. "For Yoshi, try 'cupcake kisses.' For Clyde, 'Cloud City.'"

"Kisses, huh?" Paxton replies with a smirk.

"Shut up." I face him again. "What about the interns? They'll be guarding the cliff."

"They're being trained in finance, accounting, marketing — not combat," he says. "Besides, they can't see any better than you do. Clients aside, the most dangerous part will be the stretch near the hunt starting point because of the floodlights. Otherwise, we've got the dark of night on our side. We'll move fast."

"Faster than speeding bullets?" I counter.

The closet door opens, and Cameron is standing there, chewing on a wooden toothpick. "Looking for something, children? A lightbulb, perhaps?"

Just when I'm sure we're busted, the demon winks at us and strolls off, chuckling.

YOSHI

A YETI WITH BRAIDED BANGS shoves me toward a caged Lion. I recognize her as the woman from the band flyer. Then I exclaim, "Clyde! What're you doing here?"

"We followed you to the parking garage," he replies from the next enclosure.

"We?" I echo, struggling to regain my balance. "What do you mean, 'we'?"

"Me and Aimee," the Possum says, gripping his bars.

I could just kill him. "Where —?"

The yeti fires a Taser gun between my shoulders. "Silence!"

I sink to the ground, sweat streaming. My muscles vibrate. My eyelashes ache.

"So far as I know, she's in the lodge," Clyde says.

So far as he knows. "Is she —?"

"I said, silence!" the brute reminds me. He grabs my hair and yanks my head back. "You, Cat," the yeti begins again. "You take this female as your mate."

Still in human form, the Lion snarls. If I set paw one in her cage, she'll tear me to fleshy wet pieces. "No, thanks," I say. "She's quite the hottie, but I've got my eye on somebody else." I address my next comment to the lady in question. "No offense."

The yeti lets go and tases me again.

"Frore!" calls yet another furry fiend, this one wearing round eyeglasses. "What do you think you're doing?" He's winded. These yetis live pampered lives.

"I'm asking you to reconsider your decision," Frore replies, motioning for another yeti to guard me. "Boreal, we have two male Cats." He points to Paxton, who's just arrived on the scene. "That one is even gold in animal form, but she resists —"

"I volunteer," Paxton puts in. "Least I can do, really."

What a letch.

"You were planning to breed her behind my back?" is Boreal's answer. "After I said no? You were always such a spoiled child, Frore. Did you honestly believe that because we are kinsmen, I would tolerate this act of defiance?" Without pausing for an answer, Boreal adds, "I have been too indulgent. It's past time you learned your place here."

188

To them, we're nothing more than flesh-and-bone commodities to be reproduced, kept as curiosities, and destroyed at whim. It's not the slightest bit personal. They don't care enough for that, which somehow makes the whole thing more disturbing.

The leader cleans his glasses, which have fogged from the humidity. "Toss the new Cat back into the jungle. We need to pack up and move out. The clients will arrive soon. One of them will enjoy terminating it and pay handsomely for the privilege."

Without warning, Paxton tackles me, and the yetis scatter. I catch the traitor with my claws, shredding his left eyebrow. He slams his boot into my gut. The blow sends me soaring, and by the time I've landed, Paxton has already pounced again.

With a twist, he's caught my neck in a choke hold. I recognize the move from gym class — he's a trained wrestler. Almost inaudibly, Paxton whispers, "Aimee's going to lower the sound barrier between the lodge grounds and the jungle. Once the horn blows, run for the main building. Take the stairs from the foyer down to the dock."

My back is still fried from the Taser blasts. "I don't believe—"

"Cupcake kisses," Paxton replies.

AIMEE

WHEN I ENTER the formal dining room, only Boreal and Crystal are seated at the long table, one at each end. Frore is kneeling as if before a throne.

Meanwhile, Boreal is using a napkin to furiously clean his spectacles. "For daring to question my authority in front of our brother deific and, worse, those shifter vermin, you are hereby demoted to dock security until further notice. Now, go."

Frore storms off, casting a sidelong glance at Crystal, who's added sparkly pink barrettes to her hair.

Once the door shuts, she says, "He was merely trying to help. To prove his leadership qualities by taking the initiative—"

"Help?" Boreal snorts. "Help run us out of business! If he wasn't your brother—"

"Well, he is," she replies, taking a sip of V8. "And your cousin, and . . ." She pets her furry, protruding belly. "Therefore, the uncle-cousin of your heir."

Talk about a shallow gene pool.

According to Cameron, they don't normally eat in the late afternoon. But today is special. The entire lodge is readying for the clients' arrival. Among other things, the portraits depicting Boreal have been stored away and the everywhere lime-green linens with white trim have been replaced by others in a tropical orange and red.

I deposit a plate of mutton over wild rice in front of Crystal, who cocks her head at me. "You're the English speaker. What's your name?"

I swallow hard. "Aimee."

"Ai-mee." She tries it out like a confection and reaches to feel my bicep. "This one is stronger than she looks, sturdy enough to carry a twenty-pound newborn."

I don't want to be her nanny. I don't want to be her anything.

I scurry to deliver Boreal's plate. He scoops up a hearty spoonful, hurries it to his enormous toothy mouth, and a second later shouts, "Cameron!"

The demon slips in from the kitchen and gives a punctilious bow. "You rang?"

As Boreal berates Cameron for his overabundant use

191

of salt, I take advantage of the opportunity to make a brisk retreat to the kitchen.

I'm slowly stirring the carrot pudding when the demon returns.

"You are a lifesaver!" he exclaims. "Well, not literally, because I'm immortal, and I don't care one wit about bitchy Boreal except that I am bound to his service and —"

"What do you mean by 'bound'?" I want to know.

"Conjured." Cameron scowls. "He sacrificed a yak, chanted in some long-forgotten ice language, and — *voilà* — here I am, a diabolical status symbol to impress the clientele." The horned cook trips over a cracked kitchen tile. "A pathetic purse puppy."

The relatively new lodge's workmanship is shoddy. Not only are the tiles cracked, but the windows have been painted shut, and I haven't spotted a single water sprinkler.

"It's interesting that they're willing to risk calling on the demonic at all," I say.

Cameron shrugs. "Only for show. They're not letting me do anything remotely interesting, even in the kitchen. Yak, yak, yak. Goat cheese. Yak. Yawn."

"Why you?" I ask, handing him the ladle. "What kind of demon are you?"

"Nothing fancy," he replies. "Generic hell spawn, and that's the problem. A million years go by in Lucifer's kingdom. Two million. Now we're going on three. You're assigned to torture the eternally condemned, and it sounds fun, right?"

"Uh . . ." Not really. I busy myself, fetching the bowls from the cabinet.

"So you tear off fingernails, unleash scorpions, rip flesh. But whatever you destroy grows back, so you can ravage it again and again. Sooner or later, even the most enthusiastically evil get bored." Cameron sighs. "Hell's all about connections, and I'm a nobody. I'm not buddies with any of the fallen angels or the big-name damned souls. What I wouldn't give to chat up Tomás de Torquemada or Al Capone."

"I'm sure it's rough," I say. It probably should be, being hell and all.

At the stove, Cameron strikes a meditative pose. "At least this gig is a step closer to my one true dream."

I can't resist asking. "Which is?"

The demon hesitates. "I want to be a fry cook in hell."

Sandra has declared that she'll be occasionally borrowing me from Cameron for the duration of the hunters' stay.

"Your assignment is simple," she says, tapping a feathered pen on her parquet desk. "Escort the clients around the property, leading up to the hunt. That's your job: escort. But if no one else is around and they need something to drink, fetch it. If they need some*one* to drink, fetch that, too."

I scan the itinerary, and then glance meaningfully at my ankle cuff. "You want me to take them outside the lodge?"

"Yes," she replies, holding up a key. "You'll accompany them and Cameron across the grounds to the edge of the jungle for the commencement of the hunt." Her flinch is almost imperceptible. "The demon requested you personally." The snowmen don't seem at all skittish around Cameron — quite the contrary — but Sandra does.

I make a grab, too eagerly, for the key, and she pulls her hand back. Sandra continues, "Afterward, we'll process their kills, and as for parting gifts . . ." She reaches into one of the desk drawers and sets a pair of fancy red-and-silver cups between us. "Fifteenth-century, ruby-encrusted poison chalices. An Austrian archduke used them on his grandchildren upon discovering his son's wife carried werewolf DNA."

"How clever of him," I say. They look like props for the TV show *Merlin*.

"You're not appalled?" she asks. "I feared you were a beast lover. You came into Enlightenment Alley with that Cat boy and were captured in the company of a Possum."

That is tricky to explain. "I considered their temporary companionship a necessary evil in my quest to find the she-Cat believed to have devoured my late boyfriend." I don't mention that said would-be boyfriend was himself a werearmadillo.

"Ah, now I see. That's why you were so interested in Ruby Kitahara! Last fall, a couple of cops came around the store asking about her."

At my nod, Sandra's expression softens. "Well, fear not, Aimee. All the beasts of the jungle are soon to be dead." With that, she presents me the key again.

I slide it into my anklet and turn it, and the cuff pops off.

That was easy. For all practical purposes, I just got here. It seems weird that a little good behavior and a semi-plausible lie are enough to earn her trust.

But Sandra's stressed out . . . gnawing her fingernails, picking at loose skin on her lower lip. The crease between her eyes is deeper. However uncomfortable she makes me, I'm under the impression that my presence soothes her. She wants to believe I'm on her side, or at least smart enough to fake it if that's what it takes to survive.

As I stand to leave, Sandra reaches into the drawer again and provides me with a tube of "rose beige" professional cover cream. "For those holy marks around your neck. We wouldn't want to cause our incoming guests any discomfort."

The first clients I meet are a middle-aged, human husband-wife couple, the Simons. According to Sandra, they hail from Boston and are worth over a billion dollars.

As I escort them to the welcoming reception, they chat about a daughter, Vesper (an airhead name, if I've ever heard one), who's beginning studies this winter semester at some exclusive boarding school in Vermont, and then mention giving each other matching wristwatches, each valued at a quarter million dollars, for their anniversary.

"Congratulations," I say. "How long have you two been married?"

"Twenty years tomorrow," Mrs. Borgia-Simon replies. "This excursion is the other half of our gift to each other." She loops her arm through her husband's. "We weren't much older than you are now when we first met at school. In our first-semester Alchemy and Incantations class, my mister yanked the still-beating heart out of a twelve-year-old wereotter." She gives him a quick peck on the cheek. "As he squeezed its blood into the open mouth of a demon fetus, I knew I'd found the fella for me."

I suppress a shudder. "And you sent your daughter to this same school?"

"Of course," he says, beaming and patting her hand. "Nothing but the best for my girls."

How nice. Steeling myself, I knock on the door of the second set of clients.

A vampire dressed like a rock star flings it open. He

196

tosses aside the newly drained body of one of the maid-interns and extends a bloodstained hand to Mr. Simon. "I'm Victor," he announces. "How do you do?"

As the men shake hands, I notice a necklace of what appears to be tiny human pinky bones around Victor's neck. This monster takes pride in killing children.

What will they do to Yoshi? Lower-class vamps sneer at shifter blood, and our undead guests are aristocrats. They're in this for sport. Heaven help us if they get creative.

Then again, the Simons don't seem the least fazed by the idea that they're in the presence of a supernatural predator, and that suggests they have the ability to call on malevolent magic of their own.

"My consort," Victor says, gesturing. "The scintillating Elina."

She sashays out the bedroom door of her suite, wearing four-inch spike heels and a black-and-red dress that plunges to her belly button. In my expert opinion as a Sanguini's employee, it's a clichéd choice at best.

In contrast, she seems to like the look of me. Raking her gaze up my body, Elina licks her lips with a forked tongue.

I go utterly still as she glides to nuzzle my ear.

Thinking mostly of my jugular, I point down the hall. "The reception is that way."

Elina trails a finger from my cheek to my chin and pinches it hard enough to bruise. Her eyebrows have been plucked off and painted back on, and she's missing her fangs. But those fingernails could slash my throat in a blink.

Maintaining a professional air, I address the group, "Should I not have an opportunity to say so later, I wish you a hunt to end all hunts."

Victor bounds out, clasping Elina firmly on the butt. "The hunt!" he exclaims, interrupting our standoff. "I'm so sick of cowering in seclusion. I can hardly wait!"

"Seclusion?" Mrs. Borgia-Simon repeats. "Whatever would *you* hide from?"

Abruptly forgetting me, Elina rolls her shoulders. "We chose the wrong side in the last royal coup," she explains. "Happens all the time, yet the piggish, smarty-pants eternal queen has banished us from court."

"Her enforcers are ordered to destroy us on sight," Victor puts in.

"Me, an Old Blood!" Elina whines. "I have been a treasured member of the aristocracy for centuries."

Oh, hell and damnation. I'm no demonologist, but I've picked up a bit about the undead from working at Sanguini's and the occasional hijinks that swirl around it.

Old Blood vampires are the reigning biggest of the baddies. They can enthrall potential victims, take several forms — including that of wolves and bats — dissolve into smoke, mist, dust, and shadows, and they're physically more formidable than the more newly undead. Age is a power indicator, a status marker.

Mrs. Borgia-Simon sighs. "The underworld just isn't what it used to be."

In the conference room, the first row of uncomfortable chairs has been roped off for the clients. I show them to their places and join Sandra and the other interns in back.

Suddenly, in a showy puff of rusty black smoke, Cameron appears alongside the podium, modeling flowing black robes and an imposing-looking amethyst medallion.

Opening his scaly arms wide, he grins with pointy teeth and says, "Welcome to Daemon Island. I am your host, Cameron, the demon king."

CLYDE

IT DRIZZLES STEADILY ALL NIGHT, despite Noelle's insistence that this is the dry season.

A black and blue butterfly alights briefly on my nose. It's too pretty to eat.

I have insomnia again, and the exchange over mating with Noelle put me off my appetite. With each passing hour, the world looks sharper, even with the mist. Paxton must've been mixing a mild sedative in the food, something to dull our senses.

I pick up my plate and sniff it. I can't detect anything specific, but that doesn't mean I'm wrong. I dump the gruel into the straw pile in the corner farthest from Noelle.

I gaze at her, sleeping in her hammock. Awake or unconscious, no one luxuriates like a female Cat. Every time she turns, stretches, I almost swallow my tongue. Even her soft snore is sexy, and, bonus, none of my friends has a prior claim.

When Noelle wakes up, I'm going to try shaking my cage again. Not that it did any good the last few times. These enclosures were built for far fiercer shifters than me. But I'm hopeful the storm may have swept the crutch to an edge of the roof. A matter of millimeters could make all the difference.

A cool wind blows through. It's Travis.

"Is Aimee all right?" I whisper, careful not to disturb Noelle.

Travis positions his translucent form as if he's sitting on an invisible lounge chair. "She's had a stressful couple of days, but she's hanging in there." Before I could ask anything else, he holds up a finger. "The albino Bigfoot things? As slow as you move, they're never going to toss you into a hunt."

"Meaning what?" I reply.

"Breathe," Travis says. "Nobody's going to lobotomize you or surgically alter you so you're forever stuck between animal and human form."

We've seen the same horror movies.

"But they might slaughter you and sell your pelt." Gesturing toward the next cage, Travis adds, "Not the Lion.

She's special to them. They're hoping she'll produce several cubs over the next couple of decades. Boreal hasn't given up on the idea of snagging a healthy breeding male, but he's expanded his efforts, seeking out black-market vendors of shifter sperm."

"So some rich hunters can bag the king of the jungle," I mutter. "Big freaking deal." Out loud, it sounds like I have species envy.

"It is a big deal," Travis informs me. "From what I've overheard, not even the Mantle of Dracul has a male Lion head to display as a show of strength and cruelty. Boreal could charge twice what he's asking now if there was a maned Lion in the mix."

A sliver of moonlight illuminates the curve of Noelle's haunches. "I have to get her and Aimee out of here." I caught most of what Paxton whispered to Yoshi, but I'm not about to leave the girls' lives in their incompetent paws.

Bad enough that "cupcake kisses" were Aimee's code words for Yoshi. I wonder if Travis knows that she's moving on.

Gesturing to the roof of the cage, I ask, "Where's the crutch?"

Travis points to the upper-left corner, the one opposite Noelle. "Right there."

I shuffle over, climb as high as I can, and, bracing myself with my feet, use my free hand to try to catch hold of it. "I don't feel anything," I gasp.

"You're not able to reach close enough," Travis says. "With the wind and rain . . . Maybe try again in the morning."

Sliding down, I ask, "You okay?"

Travis says, "I just wish I could do something to help."

"Be with Aimee," I tell him. "Even if she doesn't know you're there, I can't stand the thought of her being all alone in the lodge with those arctic asshats."

"Will do," the Dillo ghost replies, dissipating in the humid air.

"Who're you talking to?" Noelle mumbles in a sleepy voice. "God?"

Travis has disappeared, though he might still be listening.

"Sorry I woke you," I tell Noelle. "How do you feel?"

She yawns, stretches her arms. "Fuzzy."

I explain my theory about the food being drugged.

"That would fit with Paxton's MO," she observes, repositioning herself. Now we're face-to-face, resting on our stomachs. "When I first met him at Basement Blues, he was dealing transformeaze."

"The shift-freezing drug," I say.

She nods. "There's an underground circuit of shifter music clubs in big cities and remote honky-tonks across the countryside. I sing in this blues band, Fayard and the French Horns, and we didn't really take off until we started using. The more animal form we looked, the better

203

the audiences liked us. The money was solid, and the applause felt even better. Before long, the drug seemed necessary, and not just for business purposes."

My dad warned me about transformeaze. Except for very young adolescents and hybrids, most werepeople typically have no trouble with control during and throughout a shift. It's painful but natural, and we're still ourselves. Animal is the form, not the mind inside it.

You start toying with that . . . I can't imagine losing myself, what makes me Clyde, and going all renegade Possum. That's scary enough. But unleashing an inner Lion could get deadly fast. "Did you have issues with control?"

"That's why I stopped. Never try it, Clyde. Transformeaze is distilled from a demonic spell. Under the influence, I did things I'll always regret."

I take that to mean she did *someone* she'll always regret. I hate Paxton that much more for taking advantage of her. I search my mind for something that will reassure Noelle that I don't think less of her for what she's been through. "You're so graceful. I can barely get in and out of my hammock without fumbling all over myself."

Her lips curl. "I'm so graceful?"

"What?" I reply, blushing. "You are!" Despite the limp. I can't remember the last time I came right out and complimented somebody. I haven't even admitted to my parents that the kits are cute. "What color are your eyes in fully human form?"

"More brown, but I like them better this way. That's not the transformeaze. The various species of Cats — Lions included — tend to be better than other shifters at holding on to superficial animal-form features."

"It's worse for you here," I say. "Nobody wants to mate me to some strange Possum girl." Not that I'd necessarily mind.

Noelle props her chin on her fists. "Tell me about Possums."

I blink. "I'm not really qualified to speak on behalf of all of Possum kind."

That makes her laugh. "Then tell me about you."

So I do. We talk for hours. I tell her about Mom and Dad, Cleatus, Clara, Claudette, and Clint, about Waterloo High, working at Sanguini's, how I got hurt so badly.

Turns out she's from Atlanta, her parents work for Coca-Cola, they have a Maine coon named Aesop, and her mother collects porcelain mouse thimbles. Fascinating.

As the sun comes up, I talk about Aimee. "We'd been hanging out for a while, but after I woke from the coma, she was the person most there for me. She even tracked down VHS copies of *Galactica 1980*, plus a VCR for us to watch them on, and suffered through the whole set with me, just so I could say that I'd seen it."

"*Galactica 1980?*" Noelle repeats. "Never heard of it."

That bothers me more than it should. "I take my geek cred very seriously."

I don't get into Aimee's relationship with Travis or how he died. I'm more self-conscious about what I say now that I know he might be listening.

Besides, I don't want Noelle to think that I'm holding what Ruby did against all of Cat kind . . . because I'm not, at least not anymore.

Noelle confirms that two of her toes and a bone in her foot were broken when she was captured. "You should've seen it, all swollen up, before I could shift it partly out. It looked like a bloody stump. Paxton —"

"He's worse than those arctic asshats," I say. "Because he's a shifter, it's —"

"More personal somehow," Noelle says along with me. "I like you, Clyde. I really do. If we could ever find our way out of this hellhole —"

"We will," I promise, forcing myself up to once again try shaking the crutch from the top of my cage.

YOSHI

THE TEMPERATURE COOLS Wednesday at sunset, though last night's rain did nothing to break the humidity. The ground is muddy, messy. Cats are known for our fastidiousness. Keeping watch in a treetop, I'm cleaner and more content up high.

Helicopters come and go from the island — sometimes to drop off a shifter, sometimes for the day-to-day business of the yetis, and every once in a great while to bring hunters salivating at the chance to kill.

We're almost done setting up the Burmese tiger pits. James and Mei are digging the last one now while Brenek and Luis tweak our camouflage efforts.

I can hear Luis below, humming a blues song.

Right then Teghan scurries up the trunk, carrying half a coconut in her teeth. She hunches next to me and cradles the nut in her hands. It's filled with mashed red berries, and in the light of the rising moon, her hands are red, her face and arms decorated with crosses and doves. "Did you paint yourself?" I ask. "You're not a half-bad artist."

Taking our example, she's trying to protect herself from whatever's to come.

"I'm better at pottery," she replies. Then she hands me the makeshift bowl, stands, turns so that her back is facing me, and says, "Do the backs of my thighs."

Excuse me? "Why don't you ask Mei?" I suggest, moving so I'm no longer at eye level with her barely adolescent hind end. "I'm sure she wouldn't mind."

Teghan flashes me a grin over her shoulder. "Are you a prude or just shy?"

It's the first time I've been accused of either. "How old are you, anyway?"

The Tasmanian weredevil makes a show of rolling her eyes and swings to a limb a few feet away. "Fourteen." At my arched brow, she amends, "Okay, thirteen."

I let that speak for itself, and then she says, "Do you have an age requirement or something, like for a driver's license?"

"Or something," I reply. "Do you make a habit of coming on to older guys?"

Teghan pulls her knees to her chest. "If this is our last night on earth, I —"

I can't help laughing, and at her indignant glare, I hold up my palms in mock surrender. "I'm flattered — really. I bet you're the hottest girl in seventh grade."

"Eighth," she spits out, tapping her foot against a leafy branch.

As a peace offering, I return her half coconut of red berry mush. "Fine, eighth. But you're a little young to worry about dying a virgin."

At her stricken expression, I add, "You're not going to die, Teghan. You can't let in thoughts like that." I hold up my arm, showing off the scabbed-over wound where she bit me. "You may be a kid, but you're not some defenseless little girl, either."

AIMEE

CAMERON IS DRESSED in his usual duds, scrubbing pots and pans.

Tonight's dinner is for Sandra and the interns only. Earlier, the clients requested room service, and she said she had it handled. So I grab a towel to help the demon dry dishes, dearly wishing I was working with Clyde in Sanguini's kitchen instead.

I ask, "Where did Boreal and the other snowmen run off to?"

"Off-island," Cameron replies. "They sailed one of the yachts around to the other side for the duration of the clients' stay — except for Frore, who's still stuck babysitting the dock for mouthing off. The clientele never go there, anyway. They always take a copter in and out." At my quiz-zical expression, Cameron adds, "The deific are not about to risk revealing the secret of their existence to the clients. Sandra has 'flunky' written all over her, and besides, when marketing to maleficent sorcerers and undead aristocrats, would you rather strut out a devilishly handsome hell-spawn demon or a hirsute, paunchy evolutionary dead end?"

"Makes sense for Boreal," I reply. "But if your master is on hiatus, why do you step up at all? Why not hightail it home to hell?"

"Doesn't work that way," Cameron says. "To break the spell Boreal has over me, he has to completely abandon this island—leave with no intention of ever coming back."

I twirl a dish towel. "He does have a lot invested here."

"Tell me about it." Cameron shudders. "And please don't call him my 'master.' Some demons get off on submission, but I'm more the chaos type."

We're only minutes away from sunset. It's time for the pro-cessional to the hunt. Finally outside the lodge, I breathe in the tropical air and I take one step after another, wait-ing for my moment. I'm so nervous, I could throw up.

In contrast, Cameron is once again resplendent. He's changed into a majestic, sweeping black cape woven of mist and shadows. His fiery orange robes glide across the grounds as if the mud beneath them were polished marble.

With a flourish, he leads the clients, who're in turn

trailed by me, through parallel rows of tiki torches that stretch to the edge of the jungle.

"So tell me," Mrs. Borgia-Simon gushes. "Are you and Lucifer close?"

"Like this," he replies, holding up crossed fingers. "Me and Old Scratch, we go way back. I'm the one who pinned the tail on the serpent at his last birthday party."

"I thought Lucifer's fallen angels outranked the hell spawn," Elina muses.

I'm not sure if she's being insensitive or passive-aggressive.

I'm not sure I even care. But I can tell by the way he straightens that the remark bothers Cameron.

The demon circles back to tuck her hand in the nook of his arm before continuing on. "Alas, you don't know the inner workings of hell, sweet Elina . . . at least not yet. Perhaps tonight a werebeast will get lucky and change all that." It's the first acknowledgment that the hunt may be as dangerous to the clients as to their prey.

Mr. Simon adjusts the strap of his rifle. The missus has a gun, too, and they're decked out in classic hunter apparel. Clunky brown leather boots, night-vision goggles, various small pouches and long knives and canteens hanging off their matching belts. Topped with pith helmets, they look like theme-park safari guides.

The vamps, in contrast, appear dolled up for Goth clubbing. Elina and Victor nod to practicality only in their low heels and in covering more of their alabaster skin. For all their powers, the undead can still be cut by thorns, targeted by mosquitoes.

I'm rooting for the bloodsuckers of the tinier variety.

Mr. Simon mentions having packed silver ammo.

Victor looks surprised. "You do know that lead kills them just as dead?"

Mrs. Borgia-Simon touches up her mauve lipstick. "Even werewolves?"

Victor explains that werepeople have largely taken charge of the trade in silver weapons as a way for them to identify and track their own enemies. "It fools the amateurs. I'd think graduates of the Scholomance would know better."

Interesting. Cameron, who's gone eerily silent, has shaken their haughtiness to the point that they're sniping at each other.

Mr. Simon clarifies: "Carpathian campus," like that means something. "Are you fellow alumni?"

Elina says, "No, but I dallied with one some years ago at the gala of the late eternal king. Ravishing man, a necromancer by the name of Byron Yansky. Perhaps you know him?"

I glance at the interns standing guard on the cliff. They've ditched their lime-colored casual uniforms for paramilitary-style ones.

So far as the clients know, they're on the lookout for

any unwelcome air traffic and poised for combat in the unlikely event of an attack on the lodge grounds by any number of anti-demonic forces. Their presence, like so much of the snowmen's operation, is mostly for show. But they do know how to fire their weapons.

As the clients chat, I scan the foliage for a glimpse of Clyde's cage, finally catching sight of it only a few hundred yards from the starting point of the hunt. I should cringe at seeing him caged like an animal. I should be appalled, except . . .

"Clyde?" I whisper. How could he have bulked up like that in the few days we've been apart?

He clatters his plate across the bars, trying to get my attention. "Aimee!"

"My apologies for that unpleasant racket," I tell the clients.

Unfazed, they continue gossiping.

I spare a glance at the striking young woman situated next to my friend. She must be the captive Lion that the snowmen were talking about. She's bared her saber teeth.

I don't take it personally. I am, after all, escorting the enemy.

Mrs. Borgia-Simon remarks, "This humidity is wretched on my hair." She eyes Elina's cascading black locks. "Whoever is your stylist?"

The conversation has turned, and now they're

practically cooing at each other. I keep moving, trying to act casual. Thank heavens for their self-absorption and ADD.

"Aimee!" Clyde hollers again. It's painful, ignoring him. I only hope he doesn't think I've been brainwashed or something.

"And your nails!" Mrs. Borgia-Simon gushes. "They're works of art. Losing your humanity certainly does wonders for a girl."

Ahead, Sandra (now sporting a tropical orange suit) and Paxton have set up a lime-green silk canopy, draped over a rattan-beamed structure and decorated with bright purple-and-orange flowers at each of the four top corners.

Upon our arrival, the Cat snaps a few photos — both posed and candid — to commemorate the occasion. Then he excuses himself and marches off, probably eager, as a shifter himself, to stay as low as possible on the clients' radar.

Meanwhile, Sandra positions herself to one side, bows, and murmurs greetings to Cameron as if he has some power over her.

An owl screeches in the distance, and I take note of the intern guarding this area of the grounds from the sheer cliff. Meanwhile, the respective couples separate, each standing to one side.

From beneath the canopy, Cameron glances at the vampires. "No supernatural powers." His shifts his gaze to the Simons. "No demonic sorcery." Clasping his gnarled hands behind his back, the demon adds, "It's a battle of wits and wills, brawn and agility."

Not to mention firearms. Victor is bouncing slightly in anticipation.

Gesturing to Sandra, Cameron says, "Do fill them in on the logistics."

"No need to concern yourself with transporting your kills," she declares. "Once the hunt is concluded, we'll send out a retrieval team to fetch them. In the unfortunate event that the hunt proves fatal for one couple or the other, the surviving clients will assume responsibility for both fees in full."

I suspect the promotional brochure didn't get into that last point.

"We here at Daemon Island put a high priority on our guests' safety, albeit balanced against"— Cameron pauses for effect —"the alluring dangers that await."

Sandra sounds an air horn so loud that it's painful. "You have until dawn."

The undead aristocrats join hands and scamper toward the base of the cliff.

The human billionaires exchange a peck for good luck. Mrs. Borgia-Simon uses her hanky to wipe the lipstick off her husband. Then they strike out in the general direction of the ocean.

The hunt is on.

AIMEE

CAMERON RETREATS toward the lodge, muttering, "They're nothing but demonic wannabes, a bunch of pretentious bush-leaguers." His voice becomes mocking: " 'I once met a necromancer named Byron Yansky. He plays Parcheesi with the dead.' "

Feeling awkward, I say, "Generous of us to sound the horn. Fair warning."

"Not so generous," Sandra says as the wind picks up. "The clients would be crushed if the hunt were over too quickly. They're here to get their money's worth."

Somehow I have to ditch Sandra, and fast, without raising her suspicions. I check the cliff, and this time the nearest guard-intern is gone. With Sandra's back to him, Paxton stands in the guard's place, waving at me. Our odds just got a little better.

What was I saying? "Without using their powers or magic —"

"You're so naive." Sandra fiddles with the canopy. "Now that the clients are out of sight, they'll begin cheating immediately." She winks at me. "They are evil, after all." Scanning the skyline above the jungle, she points. "Look there."

A tiny black ribbon emerges from a trail of rising smoke and flits into the sky.

"That's Elina," Sandra says. "Even with the cover of treetops, it'll be easier for her to locate her prey from the air. Her hearing is remarkable, and she can cover more ground more quickly that way. The Simons will accomplish the same goal with a spell."

My throat tightens at the thought of the clients targeting Yoshi. My plan assumes that at least some of the jungle shifters will make it this far alive.

Sandra adds, "You'll want to change into the overalls hanging in your closet at the lodge and then wait for me at the workshop. Most hunts don't take all night. When the clients return, it'll be our job to skin the kills, cure the pelts, and mount the heads for easy transport." Apparently deciding that no amount of fiddling will make the silk

218

hang just so, she gives up. "In service to the deific, taxidermy is a rewarding, if unsavory, practice. I've grown to appreciate it."

No way am I defiling anyone's dead body.

"Well, go on," she says. "What are you waiting for?"

It's a good question. Taking a breath, I haul off and slug her in the face.

I had *no* idea it hurt so much to punch someone. I'm shaking out my hand as she falls and hits the back of her head. While she's dazed, I work as fast as I can with bruising fingers and use the canopy drape to secure her to an upright pole.

Paxton has vanished from view, and it turns out that only the closest guard-intern has been eliminated. I'm forced to mosey at an unsuspicious speed past the rest, back toward the lodge.

Fortunately, shifters have excellent hearing. As I pass Clyde and the Lion, I call, "Sit tight. I'll return for you both as soon as I can."

"Aimee!" Clyde replies. "Don't just leave me here."

I have to. Any second could be Yoshi's last. "I'll be back. Trust me."

What's more, Clyde can barely walk and he's practically worthless to the snowmen. If he becomes a problem, the interns will shoot him without a second thought.

Silently praying for Yoshi, I barrel into the empty lodge kitchen, pull out a leftover bowl of yak-potato stew, and pop it into the microwave. It's thick, hearty.

Hopefully, Frore won't taste the sedative.

I'm arranging sesame-seed crackers on a plate when Cameron rolls in. "That slutty vampire couple ripped through the housekeeping interns." He puts his hands on his hips. "The second-floor maid's entrails are hanging from a curtain rod in the sunroom."

"All the interns?" I exclaim, wondering if that's what Sandra had meant when she said she'd take care of "room service" for the clients. "They couldn't need that much blood in such a short time." Of course vamps don't redecorate with human organs because they need sustenance. They must've gotten antsy waiting for the hunt to begin.

It's the sort of thing that happens when you deprive the undead of Internet access.

Cameron taps his foot. "You, me, Sandra, and the drones standing guard are all that's left, and that, Cinderella, makes you priceless as far as I'm concerned. Someone's got to sweep the floors, change the linens, and scrub the toilets. Rumor has it that the deific's bowel movements are epically craptastic, if you get my meaning."

As the microwave beeps, I grimace at the thought. "Sandra asked me to run some stew to Frore in the security room."

Cameron takes out the bowl and sets it on the kitchen

island. "Weird. She normally does that herself," he says. "It gives her an opportunity to kiss hairy ass."

I hope he's speaking metaphorically. "Oh, um . . . she's busy —"

"Uh-huh." Cameron rests his bony elbows on the counter. "Sweetie pie, I'm a demon. I can smell deception a continent away. How 'bout letting old Uncle Cameron in on the fun? Come on, spill it. What're you up to?"

Busted. He may be attracted to chaos for its own sake, but that'll only help so much. Evil is selfish. There has to be something in it for him. I risk marching to the silverware drawer for a spoon and slip the sedative out from my bra. Then I artfully position the bowl in the middle of the circle of crackers on the square plate and stir in the sedative. "I'm going to make you a deal."

Cameron claps his hands. "How intriguing! You do know of course that making deals with a devil, even a minor one like me, is considered the exclusive territory of the criminally stupid, pathetically desperate, and utterly doomed."

Whatever. Reaching for a tray, I say, "I need a distraction, a big one, and if you can pull that off for me, I'll help you fulfill your dream of working as a fry cook in hell."

He tilts his head. "Why should I believe that *you* can do such a thing?"

"Where I come from, we have this little thing called faith."

CLYDE

"SMOKE." In the thin moonlight, Noelle's hair turns golden. "It smells like burning wood, and a lot of it. We can't stay here, caged like this."

She's right. From what Paxton told Yoshi, Aimee is going to try to lower the high-frequency barrier (Possums have good ears, too). If she succeeds, we may have serious reinforcements in the form of the other shifters. Assuming they're not all dead. I'm still barely getting around. Noelle's limping. We could use that kind of muscle.

Thank God Aimee's okay — she looks okay, anyway, at least from a distance.

I can't freaking believe she blew me off like that. I know she has someplace to be, but would she have cruised by Yoshi without stopping for a cupcake kiss? I doubt it.

"What are you doing?" Noelle asks. "What happened to your hammock?"

"Fishing," I reply. People always forget that shifters like Possums have teeth and claws, too. I've detached one of the big metal hooks used to hang my hammock, cut loose a long cord, and freed it from the woven swing. From there, I tie the rope to the hook.

As Noelle looks on, I cross to the corner where Travis said my crutch rested on the cage ceiling. I stick my arms out between the bars, wind up the rope, and yank it up and backward. The hook clangs on the top and falls back empty. I try it again, again, another twenty-two times, until Noelle says, "This is all very entertaining, but —"

I shush her. "I'm concentrating." The last time, the clang of metal on metal sounded a little different than it had all the times before.

Praying for a lucky break, I try once more, adjusting for the angle, and I feel the hook catch. I pull gently, slowly, until the crutch topples off the side and into my hand.

Within seconds, I blast through the bars. Then I half climb, half fall out onto the ground. "Stand clear," I say, and free Noelle the same way.

She leaps out, landing on her good foot, and scans the cliff. "Where did they go?"

That's strange. The two guards we can normally see from here are gone.

As I try to make sense of it, my nose itches. Vision blurs. Gut contracts.

The threat of fire, taste of freedom, curves of Noelle's butt — it's too much.

I'm losing control, shifting whether I want to or not.

"You okay?" she asks, reaching to steady me. "With your injuries . . ."

It's like her hand is on fire.

"Don't touch me," I grit out. I falter to my knees, whimpering in agony. What will she think of my bald tail? My beady eyes?

"Grow up." Noelle rips off my shirt. She breaks my jeans zipper, and tugs them off, too, ignoring my candy-cane boxers and the way that they've tented from her touch.

During our time in captivity, I've fantasized once or five times about her tearing my clothes off, but there's nothing sexual in this, at least not on her end.

It's practical. She's only trying to prevent my changing form from becoming tangled, possibly further injured, in the material.

Wracked with pain, my joints grinding, I wave her off. "The sound barrier should be down soon, if it's not already. Aimee will be here any minute, looking for us."

Noelle heard the whispered exchange between Yoshi and Paxton, too.

I point. "Wait for her between those trees. I don't want you to see me like this."

"Like what?" Noelle takes a few halting steps backward. "Clyde . . ."

"Go," I say. "G —" It's the worst, the most excruciating transformation I've ever experienced. The damage to my body must be too severe to respond naturally.

My heart thunders. My scalp prickles. My rib cage threatens to bust out of the skin.

As best I can, I take inventory. Whiskers? Check. Claws, yes, but they're enormous, and where did all this muscle come from?

My head weighs a ton. My legs — long legs? — can barely support me.

What happened to the satisfying, familiar release of my thin, naked tail?

I shut my eyes and risk inhaling, expecting my signature scent, like rotten eggs. This time, I smell blood and mud and water and sex. Or at least what I've imagined sex smells like. Noelle's scent, not mine, except . . .

The pain fades from pounding to throbbing to a faint ache. Then, as if wiped clean by the breeze, it's gone. I haven't felt this healthy and whole since before Michigan.

Did I die? Am I a ghost now like Travis?

Is that why the pain has disappeared?

I dare to open one eye, then another, staring at enormous golden-brown paws.

My enormous golden-brown paws? I curl one, retract and extend the claw.

I force myself up, first anchoring my shaking front legs, then my back.

I can't get over how I'm not sore anymore. Not at all. Not from the shift or my prior injuries. Changing form so drastically must've forced my whole system to reboot. Realign. Heal. Revealing, oh God, a part of me that I never knew existed.

The shock of it mostly retracts my shift, sparing only the body fur and whatever's left of my human face.

"Clyde?" Noelle covers her mouth. "Clyde!" She claps her hands, marveling at the change. "In human form, you smelled like a Possum." She begins laughing, a little hysterically. "You're a Wild Card shifter, part Lion. You're a Lion like me!"

"I'm more surprised than you are," I say, for the first time feeling the full weight of my proud and enormous golden mane.

YOSHI

ONCE THE HORN BLARES, my instincts urge me to flee. But Luis warned us not to expect garden-variety hunters. With the supernatural in play, there's nowhere on this island where we can't be found, and we're too far from any other landmass to swim for it.

Fine. As a Cat from landlocked Kansas, I'm not a fan of large water, anyway.

We have speed, strength, teeth, and claws, but they'll expect all that. It's our cunning that makes us unpredictable, a challenge worthy of bragging rights.

In the near darkness, I hear Luis's rumbling voice from another tree, a lower branch. "Our predecessors defaulted too much to their inner animals. We won't make that same mistake. But, as we all know, the fight-or-flight instinct is a huge shift trigger. If transforming looks like your best bet — or you can't stop it — trust in that."

He adds, "Just remember: the hunters have come for animal-form trophies. If you can avoid changing, they may not even bother firing at you, except in self-defense."

I hold my ground, or at least the tree trunk, waiting.

With their Wolf ears, I'm sure Mei and James caught all that. But they have taken point outside the ring of traps surrounding our campsite.

Each four-foot-deep pit is camouflaged with greenery and armed with twenty upright, three-foot-tall bamboo stakes, sharpened to vicious points.

"Do you see anything?" Teghan whispers.

"Not yet." Since her failed attempt to entice me with her middle-school wiles, she's defaulted to a sort of kid-sister mode. I don't mind. Someone's got to look out for her. The Bears are both good-natured guys, but I can see where their girth might intimidate her, and the newlyweds tend to keep to themselves.

"Breathe," I reply. "Use your ears, your nose."

"Are you scared?" Teghan adds. "You don't seem scared."

I've never been more tempted to fully shift. On the upside, Cats have the largest eyes of any carnivorous werepeople on land, and I've embraced my inner animal just enough to capitalize on that advantage. "Growing up, my grams used to shoot at me for fun." That's an exaggeration, but she is a gun-happy crone. "If bullets start flying, duck."

Teghan nods like it's the most original advice she's ever heard.

We sift through the noises. Mosquitoes. Monkeys. Frogs. Hogs. Rustling leaves. Wind. A bird flying overhead reminds me of Toucan Sam.

Finally, I hear footsteps, bickering, a blade slicing vegetation again and again.

"I don't see why you needed to act so chummy with them," a man remarks. "Where's your spirit of competition?"

"Did it ever occur to you that I need someone new to talk to?" a female voice replies. "We're always with the same boring people doing the same boring things."

"Really?" he exclaims. "You always stalk shape-changers in the jungle?"

"You're so mean to me. I don't know how I've stayed married to you."

Teghan whispers, "They're cocky, coming straight for us."

"They're armed," I reply. "Murder doesn't bother them. It's why they're here."

I resume listening. The husband had apparently caught his wife fooling around in the shower with one, no, *both* of the other hunters. The only other hunters.

So there are four altogether, just like Luis said to expect.

Killing them if it meant escape sounded easier before they became people to me. Even people I already don't like.

The middle-aged couple wanders into view. They're wearing night-vision goggles. He has a rifle slung over one shoulder, and she's carrying something in her palm.

A few more steps and we'll have skewered them before they can get a shot off.

I can let this happen. I have to. I have my new friends, a kid included, to think about. Besides, Aimee needs me. She never would've gotten caught up in this mess if she weren't such a fine person, if she hadn't cared enough to follow me that night to the parking garage.

"Something's wrong," the woman announces. "The arrow hasn't wavered."

Did they enchant that trinket to track us? If so, what else can they do?

"When we started out, it made sense that the compass directed us into the heart of the jungle," the wife adds. "Now it should be swinging back and forth, pausing to indicate individual creatures . . . unless they're *all* straight ahead, waiting to ambush us."

She unlatches a leather pouch attached to her belt, grabs a fistful of I'm-not-sure-what and tosses it into the air, muttering in . . . Latin, I think.

Trails of glossy-looking white smoke emerge from her palm, coil, and dance.

They hover, then spread like filmy blankets over all our traps.

I hear Teghan swallow hard as the couple gingerly approaches the border of the closest pit. The husband bends to scoop up a hefty stone and tosses it in.

It crashes through the vines and fern leaves to collide with bamboo.

As the white smoke dissipates, the husband peers in and then scans the treetops. Teghan flattens herself tighter against her branch. I instinctively do the same, angling as much of my body as possible behind the trunk.

"You're here, aren't you?" the man calls, reaching for his rifle. "All of you." He aims upward and says to his wife, "I'll flush them out."

He begins shooting, hoping to get lucky. Hoping we'll panic and show ourselves.

A bullet whizzes between me and Teghan, but we don't flinch.

Suddenly the wife charges the shooter from behind.

With outstretched hands, she shoves him into the pit.

The barrel of his gun jerks up as he squeezes off one last round.

His scream is short. Punctual.

I didn't see *that* coming.

"I know you're watching," the wife — widow — yells, walking slowly backward the way she came. "I won't try to kill you if you don't try to kill me. I didn't want to come on this stupid hunt in the first place." Retreating, she adds, mostly to herself, "I wanted to hit the menswear fashion shows in Milan and Paris. Maybe buy myself a male supermodel. Now, *that* would've been a fitting twentieth-anniversary gift."

No one moves or breathes until she's well out of human hearing range.

"Luis said the hunters were monsters," Teghan whispers. "Dead inside."

"Not all monsters are supernatural," I reply.

CLYDE

NOELLE BURIES her long, tapered fingers in my hair. "How did you not know?"

That's when it clicks — my parents' separation, how Mom's first pregnancy brought them back together. Dad isn't my biological father. Some Lion is.

Does Dad even know? Why didn't Mom tell me?

I'll have to worry about it later, if there is a later.

I turn toward the jungle. "I have to find Yoshi."

Noelle holds me back. "I thought you didn't like Yoshi."

"He's not the only wereperson out there."

"Clyde!" she exclaims. "You're a male *werelion*. Every hunter's dream trophy!"

I move to embrace her. "Then I should be able to distract them if—"

She kisses me. It's one of those deep, wet, teeth-and-tongue kisses. My first real kiss from a girl. It should suck or be awkward, but not even.

Noelle hooks a long leg around my waist, and as I grip her hips in greedy hands, she wraps herself tight around me with the other. If not for her drawstring pants, we would've gone from zero to paradise by now. It's perfect, except . . .

Breaking away, I ask, "If I were only a Possum, would you be doing this?"

"What are you talking about, 'only a Possum'? What kind of nonsense is that?" Noelle disengages her body from mine. "In point of fact, I started thinking you had real potential when you were telling me about Clint, Claudette, Clara, and Clement. I love babies. I love men who love babies."

"Not 'Clement,'" I reply. "Cleatus."

Noelle chuckles. "Cleatus. My, what a burden to put on that poor child!"

"Like 'Clement' would've been so much better," I mutter, presenting her with my electro-charged crutches. "Take these," I say, briefly explaining how to release a blast.

I don't need a weapon anymore. I've become one. And her foot is still injured.

"You know, Clyde, you ought to talk to someone about your low-self-esteem problem." Noelle tilts her perfect, smudged chin. "The fact that you're a Lion just means you'll have the stamina to keep up with me."

It doesn't matter that our buddies ditched me and Aimee to visit scenic Vermont. It doesn't even matter that I'm sans the Bone Chiller. My sidekick days are history.

AIMEE

SEATED IN A REINFORCED CHAIR in front of the console, Frore doesn't lower his copy of the *Wall Street Journal* or otherwise acknowledge my existence.

"You'll want to eat that before it gets cold," I nudge, gesturing at the stew.

Through dangling white braids, he flicks his dismissive gaze at me, if only because I'm the intern who speaks English. I'm a curiosity, like a mule who can talk.

Gripping my tray, it's all I can do not to drool over his broad shoulders at the forty-foot-long motor yacht. Do any of the shifters have nautical experience? I've heard the snowmen mention Guatemala and Costa Rica and bribing

236

government officials to look the other way. I'm not sure where we are exactly, but I suspect Paxton knows.

At least Clyde is safe in his cage, waiting impatiently for me.

Yoshi could be dead by now.

It doesn't look like Frore is hungry. I risk trying to draw him out. After all, he's the rebel, the one who's been left behind. "Why do y'all need so much money, anyway?" I ask. "Given the way humans have persecuted shifters, I understand why you'd be reluctant to go public. But what's the point of —?"

"What a shockingly sophisticated question," he remarks.

Setting aside the paper, Frore says, "That's what we call Sasquatch talk. These days, the battle for survival-of-the-fittest takes place within the world economy. We're pursuing a diversified plan, buying out major world banks, defense manufacturers, real estate. . . . We own twenty percent of Texas, and in hopes of further dumbing down *Homo sapiens*, we have underwritten the production of several reality-television shows."

"You're kidding." It just slipped out.

Frore makes a guttural huffing noise that might be a laugh.

"Cameron wanted your opinion of the stew," I prod, now that the snowman's defenses are down. "Boreal has been complaining that his cooking is too salty. The demon thinks this batch is better, and I agree, but neither of us has the discerning taste buds of your species." Somehow I manage to keep a straight face.

With a *harrumph*, Frore mutters, "Boreal complains about a lot of things."

But he lifts the bowl and slurps. Frore has big, clumsy hands, and maneuvering silverware is a challenge for him — for all of them — though Boreal insists on it in the formal dining room.

After downing the entire meal, Frore drops the bowl, licks his chops, and wipes his mouth with the back of his furry hand. Raising a finger, he says, "The level of saltiness is fine, but I recommend trying more onion, less garlic." Then he slumps to the side, unconscious.

I shove him out of my way, grateful for the chair wheels.

The console switches are labeled in the symbol-based native language of the snowmen. Unsure which controls the high-frequency barrier, I turn all of them off.

Then I fling Frore's rifle into the sea.

Throwing open the front door of the darkened lodge, I smell smoke and hear shouting. It must be the distraction that Cameron promised.

I jog toward the ocean and peer through the greenery that separates the two buildings on the compound. The guards have abandoned their cliff-top posts and set down their guns to fight a fire raging at the taxidermy workshop. Crawling between ferns, I drag their weapons into hiding beneath the huge leaves — anything to slow them down.

I consider taking a gun for self-protection, but I don't know how to use it. Besides, this isn't like playing paintball with Travis or shooting holy water at the undead. The interns are people, not monsters.

In any case, Boreal apparently didn't have a sprinkler system installed in the workshop, either. Or, for that matter, any fire hydrants on the island. So the interns are running back and forth to the beach to fill plastic buckets with seawater.

It's no use. Cameron is hell spawn, and this is demonic fire. Only he can put it out. If anything, the water is making things worse. I wonder . . . Did he enchant only that one building, or will the entire island soon be engulfed in insatiable, unstoppable flames?

YOSHI

SNARLS TURN TO YELPS. The werewolves are in trouble.

After ordering Teghan to stay hidden in the tree, I jump down, take a running start, and vault over a tiger-pit trap. I slide in the mud as I land — the wet ground is slicker than hell, and we're low on moonlight, even in those rare spots where it manages to peek between the trees.

"James!" I call. "Mei!" No answer. I hate straying too far from the kid, but . . .

"Psst," responds a melodious voice from above. At the top of a rocky incline, some fifteen feet high, the dazzling, voluptuous woman looks like she stepped out of nineteenth-century Spain. Her black veil drapes halfway

down her high-necked, long-sleeved bronze-colored gown. If she's carrying concealed, there are a lot of places to hide a weapon in that outfit.

She waves a dead woodpecker by its tail feathers. "Here, kitty, kitty!" Her other fist opens, and a black leather leash slips down. "Pretty kitty." The attached, jewel-studded collar is man-size. "Be mine? I'll stroke your fur and give you fresh treats."

She tosses me the collar, I catch it on reflex, and her cool, delicate hand suddenly covers mine. She moves fast — faster than my Cat eyes can process. Teleportation-fast.

I had no idea there was this much supernatural power in the world.

"How'd you do that?" I ask. "Where are the Wolves?"

Her eyes glint red. "You don't care. You barely know them. Tell me, kitty Cat: Is it true that you have nine lives?"

I don't know what's wrong with me. I can hear her voice, but it's a struggle to make sense of the words. "What was your name again?"

"Elina." She flings the dead bird away. "Don't like shifter blood." She pouts, reaching up to caress my cheek. "Too gamy, but you can please me in other ways."

I like the sudden feel of her in my arms, against my chest. "You're a vampire."

She wrinkles her nose. "Am not."

"Are, too." Why don't I run or fight? Why don't I *want* to?

241

"I am an eternal." She buckles the collar around my neck. "I am eternity itself."

Her fangs are missing. What's she planning to do, lick me to death?

Come to think of it, there are worse ways to die.

As I raise my claws, I'm not sure if it's to strike or tease.

The jungle melts away, and we're transported to a castle courtyard. From a distance, I hear a cello, then a string quartet. All around, I see blurred figures waltzing in formal wear. A dashing young bald man in a tux, cape, and top hat winks as he passes by.

"This is where the new eternal queen preens," Elina informs me. "One of her many residences. I do hate her so. Since the sixties, she's insisted on calling me 'Elly May.'" At my puzzled look, she clarifies: "The 1960s." Which doesn't help.

"You should have been queen. You're an Old Blood, far more exquisite and merciless than she'll ever be. And besides, she's French." Beats me what I'm talking about, but it seems to delight Elina.

She rips my shirt in two and peels the sweaty remains off my skin. Her sharp nails trail down my chest, carving bloody lines. She circles one of my nipples, and blood wells. "I'll have to share you with Victor, but you won't mind. Or at least he won't."

The waistline of my jeans doesn't faze her. Neither does

the top button. She adds, "I won't let him hurt you more than you want to be hurt."

Her fingers explore places I'm soft and hard and harder still. So do her fingernails. I feel blood streaming, soaking my briefs. I'm powerless to do anything about it. So far, it's all in fun, but if she becomes much more aggressive, I may end up a soprano.

"I'll inspect his toys," she promises. "I'll approve the when and where of teeth."

Her red lips glisten, beckon me closer. "I've never ridden a Cat," she muses, nibbling my lower lip. "In all these long years, I've never —"

A blow knocks us both off our feet, and a familiar voice commands, "Get your forked tongue off my precious baby brother, you ungodly arrogant whore."

YOSHI

THE COURTYARD DISINTEGRATES … the castle, the classical music, and the elegant dancers. I'm in the island jungle again. No, I never left.

Elina's face turns furious, like a gargoyle. She vanishes into mist.

Not that she matters. My savior has my undivided attention. She's painted red wings on her arms and shoulders, an eye on her forehead, dotted her nose, and drawn whiskerlike lines from its tip to either side.

The effect is otherworldly. Is she the sister I've always loved, a murderous temptress, or some ancient Egyptian goddess, newly reborn?

Wincing, I sit up. "Ruby? My God, Ruby, it *is* you!"

How long has she been on the island? Was she watching me — watching over me — this whole time? I wonder if she really murdered the Armadillo boy, whether she knows the Dillo royal family has a price on her head, and why she never mentioned being a secret agent. I want to tell her how worried I've been, and how relieved I am to see her alive. Instead, I say, "Thanks, but I was holding my own with that one."

Ruby hauls me to my feet. "She had you in her thrall. And just FYI, that walking corpse is a soulless, psychopathic serial killer who'll not only drain you dead but, just for fun, harvest the gelatin from your bones to make Jell-O shots."

"You've studied demonology?" I ask.

"And seen a lot of monster movies," Ruby replies, pulling me into a hug. Unbuckling the jeweled collar from my neck, she adds, "I cannot believe you left Grams at home alone with Wilbur!"

I wish to God I'd found Ruby anywhere else. "Wilbur's fine," I say. "He has more friends in Butler County than the both of us put together."

It's true. He's a popular pig, a blue-ribbon winner. He got his picture on the front page of the *Butler Eagle* and everything.

A roar explodes in the night — another.

"Werebears?" Ruby mutters, dropping the collar.

We're off. Her stride is shorter, but she's just as fast. She's been training.

"Careful," I warn. "We dug pits—"

"I know," Ruby assures me, darting between two skinny trees. "I saw."

On the opposite side of camp, the werebears loom, enormous in full animal form. I can't tell which one is Luis and which one is Brenek.

Standing on hind paws, gripping each other's shoulders, in the dark, they almost look like they're dancing. But with snapping, bloodied teeth, there's no mistaking the growls for play. One has a bloody patch where his ear used to be.

"Cut it out!" I yell, trying to push them apart. "Brenek! Luis! What's wrong—?"

A front leg lashes out, knocking into my chest. Ruby catches me in midair.

"Do not insert yourself into the middle of a werebear fight," she scolds.

"You can't tell me what to do!" I exclaim, rubbing the already-sore spot where I was struck. "They're not fighting. Or at least they shouldn't be. They're friends."

Brenek and Luis careen over, and that's when I see red smoke hovering over them. "They're ensorcelled," Ruby whispers. No need to kill us if we kill each other.

Scooping up a stone, I weigh it in my hand. I have to break the spell, like Ruby did with Elina and me. But as I pull back my arm to throw, Ruby says, "It's too late."

One of the Bears is dead.

As the smoke thins out, the survivor roars in anguished surprise. When it's clear he won't turn on us next, I drop the rock and it lands with a thud.

Bones crack, and thick, dark hair retracts, finally revealing Brenek.

Which means the Bear-form body on the ground must be Luis. Must have been Luis.

Still mostly covered in fur, Brenek chokes out, "I don't . . . How could I —?"

"It's not your fault," Ruby insists. "They're using magic to manipulate us."

Brenek's nude, now man-shaped form is covered in oozing claw marks. But he can't take his eyes off the friend he just slaughtered. "It's not impossible to break a spell if you have enough willpower. Something I'm apparently short on."

"Luis could've killed you just as easily," I reply. "You can't blame yourself."

"It's not that simple," Ruby says at the same time. When Brenek remains frozen in place, she slaps him hard across his bleeding face. "Torture yourself later," Ruby suggests. "In the meantime, we need you."

It's tough love, and it works. Brenek notices her for the first time. "You're here."

I recall that they know each other from the interfaith coalition he told me about.

Glancing my way, Ruby asks, "What's the plan?"

My sister's never been one to defer to me, though she used to always ask my opinion. It's nice to see that hasn't completely changed, even if she has been living a secret life. I say, "We have to find Teghan and the Wolves. Then make a run for the lodge and down to the dock. The hunters are a deadly distraction. We can't keep letting them suck us in. All that matters is that we get to freedom and that nobody else dies."

Right then, Teghan, screeching, bursts into the clearing with James and Mei snarling at her heels. "Yoshi!" she yells. "Somebody, help!"

I don't understand. Why're they so pissed at the kid? Are they enchanted, too?

As the Wolves pass, Brenek snags one and rips off its head.

"No!" I exclaim, swooping Teghan in my arms. "Brenek's losing it again." I lift her onto the nearest overhanging limb so she can catch her breath.

Ruby breaks a smaller branch off the tree behind me. "No, he's not!"

The decapitated wolf-shaped body morphs seamlessly into human form, a fully clothed man, and not James. I've never seen the guy before.

He falls in two pieces onto the jungle floor. It's like a glamour has been ripped away.

The second werewolf—no, *vampire* in wolf form—

reveals herself as Elina. She's not winded. There's not a long, dark hair out of place. Her gown isn't even wrinkled.

"Darling, foolish Victor." Glaring at Brenek, she says, "Bad Bear."

Then she lifts the head of her formerly undead — now *dead* dead — partner by his spiky hair and kisses it on the lips.

Meanwhile, Ruby raises her improvised stake.

I whisper, "Don't look into her eyes."

"I'm not an amateur," my sister replies. "While you've been on the farm, I —"

"Haven't I seen you somewhere before?" Brenek asks Elina, interrupting our bickering. "I'm talking Chicago. North Shore." Despite everything, he smiles. "The castle courtyard. I was in Bear form. . . ."

I can't help wondering if it's the same courtyard Elina showed me while I was enthralled. "Excuse me," I pipe up. "Do you two know each other?"

Elina's jaw drops. She recoils from Brenek, tosses Victor's head like a hot potato, and, hissing, dissolves into mist. My sister and I gape at the Bear for an explanation.

"Chicago's a tough town" is all he'll say.

CLYDE

NOELLE WOULD BE FASTER in animal form, on three good legs instead of one, but if she'd come along, her injury still would have slowed me down. So she's scouting out the grounds, guards, and fire, strategizing our way through the lodge.

Meanwhile, I'm tracking a hunter. If not for the handgun, it'd be hard to take her seriously. Remove the nightvision goggles, and she could be any suburban mom playing Mrs. Great White Hunter for Halloween.

I run a big tongue over big teeth, feeling every inch the jungle king.

I love it so much that I let the hunter get a shot off.

"Yoshi!" shouts a female voice, and someone else says, "Get down!"

I can't see them through the plant life, though I never had such fantastic vision before tonight.

Is Yoshi dead? Aimee will be heartbroken if the Cat doesn't make it out alive.

"Don't move, or I'll shoot!" the hunter calls. "I mean, I'll shoot again."

"Liar," a rumbling voice taunts. "You said the hunt meant nothing to you."

The woman takes cautious steps. "No need to take it so personally. I just want to bag a head or two before taking off to Cabo, if only to prove I was here."

As she raises the gun again, I pounce, using muscles that are new to me. I have no thought but to stop her from hurting anyone else.

My front paws strike her shoulder blades, sending her flying. She somehow falls *through* the ground, screaming, and then goes deathly silent.

Mystified, I tentatively explore the surrounding mud and undergrowth with my right front paw, testing for quicksand. Hunkering low, I feel more Possum than Lion as I creep to the edge of a previously camouflaged pit. What with the wooden spikes protruding from her broken body, the woman looks like a giant, grotesque voodoo doll.

Navigating around the pit, I move toward where the shifters' voices came from.

I didn't mean to kill the hunter. I've never want to kill anyone, except maybe . . .

"Yoshi," a feminine voice says again, this time more gently.

I raise my Lion's head to face Travis's murderer, the infamous Ruby Kitahara. She's with her brother and a huge, naked guy that I've never seen before.

A girl drops down from a branch and tells Yoshi, "You were supposed to duck."

His side is bleeding. "Next time," the Cat promises. "Don't worry. It's not bad."

Ruby rushes to check on him. "It's not good either. The bullet only grazed you, but . . ." She gingerly examines the wound, and he hisses.

"You've probably broken ribs," Ruby says.

He'll live. It's not like blood's pouring out.

I've been hurt way worse than that.

The younger girl peels off her T-shirt, which is no big deal, given that her sports bra covers more than the average bikini top. She offers it to Yoshi. "Use this."

"Thanks, Teghan." He applies the pressure himself, waving off his hovering sister.

Makeshift hammocks. The remains of two — no, three — fires. The bones of a large hog. This must be where they made camp.

The hog hasn't been dead that long. There's still meat on the carcass. I salivate, briefly wondering if Lions scavenge.

The Bear greets me: "Nice to meet you, man."

"He must've been hiding in the jungle, too," the kid puts in.

"If the sound barrier is coming down, it should be down by now," Yoshi says. "We've got to move. Where are the real Mei and James? And for God's sake, Brenek, find something to cover your junk with. Teghan and my sister are standing right here."

"Not that I'm looking," Ruby assures him. "Or interested in looking."

"It's the principle of the thing," Yoshi insists.

"I'm looking," Teghan pipes up.

The Bear rips down a hammock, yanks out the bark, and secures what's left by tying together the vines at his side, over his right hip. "The Wolves are supposed to be waiting for us at the jungle's edge, across from the lodge. That was the plan, right? Avoid getting tangled up in the hunt and make a beeline out of here?

"We have to go with it. And fast. That overdressed vampire bitch might double back after us like the human woman did."

It's nothing but noise. I've found my prize. Ruby is scraped, body-painted, and wearing a thrashed T-shirt that falls mid-thigh. She looks every inch like sex personified.

I hate myself for still finding her attractive.

Ruby sniffs at me. "What're you waiting for? A Courage Medal?"

It doesn't matter that I'm outnumbered. Or that I don't know how many other death pits they've rigged. Or the more global insanity that seems to permeate every inch of this island. All I can think about is Travis and the way he died.

Throwing back my head, I roar. It's the loudest noise I've ever made.

I relish the flash of fear in Ruby's green eyes.

The Bear holds up a steadying hand. "Take it easy, man."

Ignoring him, I attack. Ruby dodges to the side, grabs a branch, and pulls herself out of reach. Can Lions climb trees? I'm about to try following her up when Yoshi throws himself between me and the trunk.

"Go on," he orders the others. "Brenek, take Teghan. We'll catch up."

"Yoshi!" the girl protests. "You're hurt —"

Brenek tosses her over one shoulder and, ignoring her screeching, jogs off.

Yoshi begins again, this time addressing me. "I don't know if you're ensorcelled or just a random asshole. But that's my sister you just lunged at, so unless you want to take me out, too — and God, I'm in no shape to fight a *Lion* — show your human-form face and tell us what the hell is wrong with you. Now."

If I hurt Yoshi, Aimee will never forgive me, especially since he's already injured and being all noble and annoying in the face of probable death. Jerk.

It's total BS that I'm self-conscious about retracting the shift. I can hear my bones grind, feel fluids leaking. There's a flash of pain.

By the time it's faded, I'm soaking wet and shaking and a whole lot less threatening to look at. Being butt naked, too, only makes me feel more vulnerable.

At least some of the muscle I'd picked up from Lion form has stuck, and though it's hard to tell in the moonlight, I'd swear my once salt-and-pepper body hair is now tinged a golden brown.

"You look taller," Yoshi finally says, almost keeping the shock out of his voice. "You *are* taller — two inches, maybe three." He frowns. "Does Aimee know about this?"

Before I can reply, Ruby calls from above, "Um, hello? What's going on?"

My gaze searches the treetops, zeroes in on her shadowy form. "My name is Clyde Leonard Gilbert. You killed Travis Reid, and I'm here to make you pay for it."

Ruby snaps her fingers. "You're that other dishwasher from Sanguini's." She executes a midair flip on the way down. "You think *I*—"

"The Armadillos . . ." Yoshi puts in. "A *lot* of people in Austin think it was you. Travis's family put a price on your head." He adds, "By now it's on mine, too."

"I didn't do it," Ruby insists. "I tried to save Travis." She pauses, frowning up at her younger brother. "I wasn't the only Cat-form shifter in the park that night."

255

Yoshi asks me, "How do you know it was Ruby?"

Come to think of it, Travis never said that he *saw* Ruby attack him, only that he was sure it had been a Cat that pounced him from behind. What with everything else that was going on at the time and her being on the scene and in the thick of it, we all assumed . . . But there was another local Cat, prowling for shifters, the one whose fault it is that we're all here. "Paxton?"

"Paxton," Ruby agrees in a hollow voice.

AIMEE

I JOG THROUGH the tiki torches, toward the cages, eager to free Clyde, and run into a Cat fight. Paxton spits blood. "You worthless junkie, Noelle!"

"You dealt it!" she counters, pointing a crutch I recognize as Clyde's.

"I'm a businessman." Paxton replies. "If you couldn't handle —"

"Hey!" I exclaim. "Powerful werepredators! News flash: The interns are distracted by the pretty fire. Nobody's guarding the dock. How about you secure our yacht, figure out where on earth we are, and do *anything* more useful than this?"

"Duck," Noelle shouts at me.

I do, and she blasts electricity from the crutch, leveling a gun-wielding guard-intern, who falls to the ground behind me.

"Was that necessary?" I exclaim.

"I thought so," Noelle replies.

"Definitely," Paxton adds.

At least they've found something they can agree on. "Are those Clyde's crutches?" I ask. "Where —?"

"Clyde will return with the other shifters at any moment," Noelle assures me as Paxton hauls the unconscious, possibly deceased, guard into the nearest bushes.

"Return?" I exclaim. "You mean he went *into* the jungle?"

Ignoring me, she raises her nose. "The fire is spreading."

I believe Noelle that Clyde escaped his cage, but I feel compelled to double-check anyway. No Possum. I continue alone toward the canopy, where the hunt began.

My first thought is that Sandra, still secured to one of the poles, blacked out, but there's something empty about her stillness.

"Are you my consolation prize?" a cloying, feminine voice inquires.

It takes a moment to locate Elina in the low moonlight, beyond the torches, now that the floodlights are out.

She wipes what's likely Sandra's blood from her lips,

and I recall with a gulp that the tattooed crosses that once protected me are now covered by rose-beige concealer.

"What a wretched night!" Elina whines. "The hunt was boring, I lost my Victor, and some cocky werebear is apparently stalking me around the globe. I doubt that even ripping out your squishy heart will make me feel better. I have half a mind to drown my sorrows in a bottle of holy water."

Half a mind is too generous an assessment in my opinion. But before I can choke out that parting thought, the tip of a bamboo spear bursts out of her chest. Her bloody lips turn to soot, her thin nose disintegrates, and her long black hair blows wild before she collapses into dust at my feet. The wind catches and disperses what's left of her.

Strong arms lift me in a fierce embrace. "Yoshi?"

Clyde steps away, holding me at arm's length.

Or at least I think he's Clyde. If I didn't know better, I'd swear I'm looking at an older brother that I know he doesn't have. Clyde's wearing a sort of skirt made of leaves and vines, and sporting a newly defined set of shoulders, arms, pecs, abs, legs . . . and whatever's *under* that skirt.

Not that I'm superficial. Not that I'm gawking.

Okay, I'm gawking.

He grins. "I hate that arctic-white hair color on you."

So do I. "Nice outfit," I reply, reminding myself that most shifters are more comfortable showing skin than most humans. Still, there's a lot of beefcake on display.

My gaze moves to a likewise half-naked Yoshi. "What happened?"

At that moment, Clyde stops touching me, and I miss the feel of his hands.

"Bullet," Yoshi replies, holding a wad of bloody material to the wound. "It didn't hit anything that won't heal fast."

The Cat's steady on his feet, but that had to have hurt. I hope he's not just being brave.

Meanwhile, a big guy, dressed like Clyde, sets down a thoroughly pissed-off tween girl in shorts and a training bra. He introduces himself as Brenek, her as Teghan, and the more put-together couple with them as Mei and James.

Another young woman steps forward. Recognizing her from pictures, I say, "You must be Ruby Kitahara."

Yoshi moves to my side and wraps a possessive arm around my shoulders. "Ruby didn't kill your friend Travis," he announces, almost gleefully. "Paxton did."

AIMEE

FIERY GROUNDS SEPARATE US from the lodge. The flames stretch from the sheer, soaring rock wall on one side to the ocean on the other. The fire is orange and yellow, filled with curling dark shadows. Clyde breathes Noelle's name, and Yoshi mutters, "On the bright side, if there's any air traffic nearby, our smoke signal's a lot bigger."

Then Cameron calls, "Hey, kids." He skips toward us through the blaze like it barely tickles, wearing blue jeans and a tight T-shirt that reads: HORNY LITTLE DEVIL.

"Cameron!" I exclaim. "What were you thinking? Are you trying to burn down the whole island?"

"Bad news, sweetie pie." Ignoring my criticism of his handiwork, the demon crosses his scaly arms over his

261

thin chest and says, "The human sycophants are in retreat mode. They've already captured and loaded Noelle and Paxton onto the yacht. They're giving the clients another three minutes to show." He glances at his Swatch. "Make that a minute and a half. Then they're out of here."

Taking our last chance of freedom with them.

"The hunters are all dead," Yoshi replies.

Brenek asks, "You're friends with a demon?"

Not exactly. "How was I supposed to know he's a pyromaniac?"

"He's a demon!" Ruby exclaims. "Have you not heard of hell*fire*?"

"He's a demon?" Teghan echoes. "That's awesome."

"No, it's not," Yoshi scolds.

"Werepeople!" I exclaim. "Will you please give me one minute to think?"

We could retreat into the jungle, try to outrun it. But this is an island. There's nowhere to go. The beach maybe, but without shelter . . .

Besides, the fire will just keep coming. We have to make this work somehow.

I step, nose-to-nose, facing Cameron. "You cast the spell that sparked this inferno. You can put it out." He doesn't look impressed. "Uh, would you please put it out?"

"Excuse me," he replies. "I believe you owe me something in exchange for this . . ."— he waves his arms in the direction of the building inferno —"distraction."

I reach into my skirt pocket. "You mentioned that connections are important in the underworld."

"It's a lot like earth that way," Cameron says. "All about who you know."

I offer him my business card from the restaurant. "When you get home, give this to a tall, smarmy dude who answers to the name Bradley Sanguini. If hell has a kitchen, he's the one running it. Tell him we vouch for your cooking skills."

Cameron squints at the card. "You're saying the dude's a player? Downstairs?"

I have to make this good. "I'm saying he managed to revive the essence of Dracula Prime and nearly brought on a worldwide, Carpathian-level undead apocalypse. Clyde and I almost died, banishing Brad and the Count to hell. I'm talking über-ambitious evil and creative about it, the kind of big bad they write sonnets about. Plus he's the ultimate foodie, you know, for someone who never eats solids."

"And *you two* sent this guy and Count Fabulous to hell?" the demon presses.

That might be overstating it. "Well, it was us"— I gesture at the Possum who's staring at me like I've lost my ever-loving mind—"and a few friends of ours." I hope they're *enjoying* that Vermont vacation. "Actually, Clyde and I were the sidekicks."

"That's so cool! I aspire to be a sidekick someday." The

demon slips my card into his back pocket. "Or minion, whatever."

He rubs his hands together eagerly. "All right, sweetie pie. It's a little unorthodox — to say the least — but I'm going to take this one on faith." Cameron gestures with a gnarled, clawed finger at the fearsome fire, and a clear path appears, leading to the lodge. "Hurry before I change my mind."

"Run!" I yell, praying that he's not toying with us.

Clyde sweeps me up and leads the others through the charred corridor, surrounded by flames. He's fully healed, but it's more than that. I can't imagine he's ever moved this fast before, and he's carrying himself like an Olympian.

I'm about to say so, when he asks, "Why Yoshi and not me?"

"What?" The heat is blistering from both sides.

"I get that you think he's robust-looking," Clyde continues. "But we've been through a lot together. So I think I deserve to know: Why did you send Paxton with your plan and code words to Yoshi but not me?"

Oh, for God's sake. "I told Paxton to talk to *both* of you." The Cat probably figured a physically challenged wereopossum wasn't worth the effort or else Clyde somehow pissed him off, but there's nothing I can do about that now. "Your code words were 'Cloud City.' "

Behind us, Yoshi is bringing up the rear of the group,

his hand pressing against his side. Ruby slows to keep pace with him, ready to catch her brother if he goes down.

"Cloud City?" Clyde grins. "Because Calrissian had an escape plan, even though he had no choice but to pretend to work with the Imperials, just like you in the lodge."

"Obviously," I reply, loving that he so totally gets me.

As the path disappears behind us, Clyde gently deposits me on the front step. "This may sound like a weird question," I begin. "But did the snowmen do any dental work on you?"

"Don't think so," he says. "Why?"

I reply, "Your teeth look different." Bigger.

With his back to a raging wall of fire, a winded Yoshi mutters, "If they're at the dock, we may be able to take them by surprise."

Ruby reaches for the knob. "Locked."

In no mood to mess around, Brenek simply shoves the door down. The rest of us half dive, half fall inside after him. I hear a cough and an exclamation in Spanish. They've managed to get the lights back on.

In the smoky foyer, the guard-interns greet us at gunpoint, some from the stairs leading up. The one at the top makes the sign of the cross.

How many of them are here only because they were desperate for a way to send money home to their families? They look young, terrified. I think of their friends who were slaughtered by the vampires — anything to accommodate the clients. The interns are as much captives here as we are. Which in no way means they won't shoot us.

Teghan realizes aloud, "We should've climbed *over* the building to the dock."

Clyde steps forward with his hands in the air. "Let the others go, and I'll surrender without a fight. Otherwise, you'll have to kill us all, and what a waste of an investment. I'm a male Lion. There's nothing that your masters prize more. Think about it: a hunt with me as your leading man? We're talking a freaking fortune."

What on earth does he think he's doing? "You're crazy!" I yell as one of the interns struggles to translate what he just said into Spanish for the others. "Clyde —"

"Shut up, Aimee!" he replies.

Is that his idea of last words? I know what the interns are thinking. There may be only one yacht at the dock, but they could always release us, let us have the boat, and radio the snowmen for pickup.

I open my mouth to protest that Clyde's lying and a goofball and a wereopossum and it barely makes sense that he's able to walk, let alone run with the predators, when his eyes turn burnished gold.

CLYDE

A GUARD UP FRONT waves my fellow shifters toward the downward stairs. Brenek takes Teghan and goes. I sense that if it weren't for the kid, he would've fought me on this. But it's like we have an unspoken agreement to protect her.

The Wolves follow, but Aimee stays because of me, Yoshi because of her, and Ruby because of him. I don't have time to indulge their BS heroics. "Yoshi." I wince against the coming shift. "Do me a favor. Take Aimee and your sister out of here."

"It's what he wants," Yoshi tells me.

"We should hurry," Ruby adds.

"Clyde, no!" Aimee exclaims as the Cats drag her off. "You can't!"

I try to tell Aimee it's the only way, but my throat muscles expand to accommodate a thicker neck, and my mane pours out. Now I can't talk at all.

As my hands and feet transform into paws, I catch a last glimpse of Ruby, disappearing down the stairs. I wasted so much energy hating her.

The air cools, and some of the smoke swirls into Travis, who seems to be trying to manifest. I don't know what he's up to, but I do the only thing I can think of to buy him time.

In Lion form, I collapse in a limp heap and roll my eyes back, playing dead like only a Possum can. For a moment, the guards are stunned.

Then a gravelly version of Travis's voice announces, "I am the spirit of Daemon Island." He drops his jaw open wide like a wraith, creating a vortexlike visual effect. "Your lives belong to me."

The guards flee, shrieking — some upstairs, some down the hall — as he bellows again, I think repeating the same thing in Spanish.

Not that I blame them. Travis is terrifying.

Wow, he's having fun.

As his haunting form swirls above the foyer, I roll to my paws and bound downstairs toward the dock.

It's dawn. Only one unconscious arctic asshat and the lifeboats remain.

Peering out to sea, I spot two larger vessels. Which one

is under the command of Aimee and the shifters? Which one is carrying the hairy SOBs?

Travis won't be able to hold off those nutjobs upstairs forever, and they're still armed. It'll take too long for me to shift back to human form and paddle out to either boat.

I don't have a choice. I sprint toward the ocean, take a deep breath, and launch myself into the water, praying that werelions can swim.

YOSHI

JAMES KNOWS SOMETHING about driving a boat, or at least he's faking it well.

Brenek is busy freeing the female Lion, who was already chained and loaded for transport when we boarded. So was Paxton. We're leaving him like that and letting Teghan yell and spit at him.

I hear Mei call, "Ruby, come give me a hand with the radio!"

My sister rushes in past me from the deck. I replace Teghan's now-bloody T-shirt with a fresh towel from the closet. Holding it to my gunshot wound, I take

Ruby's place, standing watch from the rail. I meant it when I told her I wasn't hurt that badly. I expect the bleeding to stop soon, now that I'm not running around anymore.

The yetis' yacht is closing in on us. A small fleet of lifeboats, carrying the armed lackeys, is floating slowly in our direction. The lodge is consumed in flames.

God, my side hurts.

Aimee joins me on deck. "You should go lie down. There's no reason to . . ." Pointing out at the water, she shouts, "Clyde?"

Of course, Clyde, and just when I was starting to look forward to comforting Aimee over her latest loss. He's swimming in Lion form. Or at least dog-paddling. "James!" I call begrudgingly. "We have to pick up Clyde."

A gunshot sounds from the yeti boat.

Pulling Aimee low, I say, "Get back inside! Tell James where Clyde is!"

The yetis have spotted him, too. They veer after Clyde as two enormous dorsal fins break the water's surface. The yetis shoot at the enormous sharks (at least I think they're sharks), trying to protect their prize.

A furry white figure leans over the rail, aiming his rifle.

Then a killer whale — no, a *wereorca* — explodes from the water and captures the shooter in its massive jaws. He's a goner. The rifle plummets, and together they careen back into the ocean with a bloody splash.

"Detective Zaleski's on the radio," Aimee hollers from the cabin. "Look up!"

In the distance, I spot the incoming helicopter.

The yeti boat is retreating at maximum speed.

We're saved.

CLYDE

THOUGH I NEVER BLASTED ANYONE with my crutches, they still helped save my life. Nora equipped them with tracking devices. Only glitch? The moisture on the island dampened the signal, or she and the other grown-ups would've rescued us sooner.

I felt hugely badass about my Lion form until running into those wereorcas. They scared the pee out of me. But once I realized they were on our side, I was actually relieved when one surfaced beneath me for transport to the shifter-controlled yacht.

Meanwhile, between the ocean attack and incoming copter, the arctic asshats bailed, abandoning their college-age henchmen, who've all been checked into an interfaith coalition debriefing facility in Mérida by now. From what I understand, most of them had no idea what they were getting into when they signed on with Sandra. It was definitely one of those too-good-to-be-true deals.

We spent our first evening off Daemon Island at a four-star resort on Peninsula Papagayo. Everyone else ate and hit the sack while Zaleski brought in a werecondor healer, vacationing from Long Island, to treat Yoshi's wounds.

Our plane landed in Austin yesterday afternoon. The werewolf couple — Mei and James — continued straight to Orlando. Nora replaced their tickets, finagled new resort-hotel reservations, and presented them with a check for ten thousand dollars. We all signed the wedding card. That Nora, she's got cash and style.

Teghan is home again, living the quiet suburban life with her family in Northwest Austin. Yoshi mentioned something to her parents about anger counseling, but she'll be all right. The kid's a marsupial. Feistiness comes with the territory.

This afternoon, the cops delivered Paxton to Travis's grandfather. It wasn't their regular protocol, Zaleski explained. But Richards has labeled the crime an assassination, and he has certain rights as a king. Not surprisingly, Paxton's been whining that he was set up and that we should take into account his help in getting us off the island he freaking brought us to in the first place. The good news is he'll never hurt anyone again.

274

Tonight Father Ramos and the detectives are meeting with Ruby at Nora's house, and Aimee and Yoshi stayed to speak in her defense.

Ruby may not have murdered Travis, but there's still the matter of the cops she killed while undercover with the vampire Davidson Morris.

I told my parents the truth, everything except about my newfound Lion form and being haunted by Travis, who hasn't made an appearance since the lodge. I'm surprised Mom and Dad let me out of the house. But it's Saturday night, and I have a date.

Noelle decided to chill out for a couple of weeks in Austin — she and Brenek are organizing a memorial concert in honor of their friend Luis, who didn't make it off the island. Tonight she's meeting me for dinner at Austin's finest barbecue joint.

I'm cruising in the Bone Chiller, jamming to the latest Screaming Head Colds tune on the radio, when a hollow voice next to me asks, "Where are you going?"

"Gah!" I shout, nearly colliding with a pickup truck as I come around a curve on Mount Bonnell. "Travis! You could've killed me!"

"This is an ugly, freaky car," he says. "It gets lousy gas mileage. You should bury it and let the domino bones rest in peace."

"You hate it that much?" I ask. When Travis doesn't reply, I add, "You okay? Is the archangel pissed at you?"

When he showed himself on the island, my Dillo pal broke his promise to haunt only me, even if it was to save my life.

Travis's vaguely blue form flickers. "I did get chewed out. But the angel gave me an extension. This is my last day to make things right."

I don't get it. His murder is solved, and Paxton was delivered to his grandfather. What's left to fix?

Before I can ask, he says, "You need to break up with Noelle."

Wow, he's gotten awfully bossy in his afterlife. "Forget it. She's the best —"

"You're gaga over Aimee. You have been since before I died, but you're too good of a friend to do anything about it, before or after. I appreciate that, by the way."

"What? I'm not gaga —"

"Admit it. You're latching on to Noelle because, unlike Aimee, you consider her available. Fair game. But it's time, Clyde. I'm not just giving you permission. I'm telling you to get your butt in gear before Yoshi or somebody else swoops in and it's too late."

The neon sign for Bette's Barbecue is blinking just ahead. "Noelle —"

"Is sexy, sultry, and a Lion to boot, but you barely know her. It's a fling built on shared danger, a common enemy, pheromones, and your own guilty conscience. Do you honestly think Noelle has any idea who Qui-Gon Jinn is? Or digs late-night games of D&D?"

I hit the brakes and signal to turn. "There's more to life than D&D."

"Always the smartass," Travis replies as cars whiz by. "But I'm here to tell you, the big picture looks different from the other side. You don't know how much time you have left. Nobody does. I pussyfooted around and lost my chance with Aimee. So answer me this: If you thought you had a real shot at being with her, you know, boyfriend-girlfriend, knowing I'd be okay with it, which girl would you choose?"

I pound the steering wheel. "What if Aimee doesn't choose me back?"

As Travis begins to dematerialize, his last word to me is "Courage."

AIMEE

FATHER RAMOS INSISTS this isn't a formal hearing, just a conversation over dinner in Nora's family room. The chef herself is at Sanguini's, but she left us a heaping bowl of her famous West Texas rattlesnake ravioli marinara and fresh bread. Neither of the Kitaharas has touched a bite, which says a lot about how tense they are.

Zaleski and Wertheimer apparently suspected Paxton of killing Travis all along, even more so after they confirmed two sets of Cat DNA at the murder scene, though they didn't have a sample of Paxton's to compare. Plus it turns out that they had their own contacts at the interfaith coalition and had confirmed Ruby's status as an operative.

She got in too deep and killed a cop to protect her cover. That's tragic and a huge deal, especially to the detectives. But it was also Ruby who passed on the information to Quincie that Bradley Sanguini (the chef I referred Cameron to in hell) had infected hundreds of diners (including me) with demonic blood by mixing it into one of the restaurant desserts: the chilled baby squirrels, simmered in orange brandy, bathed in honey cream sauce. Tasted better than it sounds.

I conclude, "That knowledge opened the door to our finding a way to defuse the supernatural contaminant, so that none of those guests ever manifested as vampires. Without her, we'd never have known to try to stop it."

I don't mention that *I* was one of the infected, but I'll thank Ruby privately later.

She exhales. "All this time, I thought I had failed completely."

From the head of the table, Father Ramos sips from a glass of merlot. "Ruby, you're not the first undercover agent who found herself faced with an impossible choice. But you might benefit from more structure than the coalition provides our operatives."

Her cautiously hopeful expression falters. The work means so much to Ruby. I've seen evil — demonic evil — up close. I respect the people who step up to fight it.

Zaleski's already put away half a heaping plate of pasta. "Ms. Kitahara, we have a lot in common. Neither of us

279

likes playing by the rules when they get in the way of the right result, but it's all about knowing *which* rules to break and why."

"What're you saying?" Yoshi asks. "She feels awful about —"

"I'm asking Ruby . . ." Zaleski replies, shooting a warning glance at her brother. "I'm asking Ruby if she's ever considered a career in law enforcement."

YOSHI

RUBY IS STILL TALKING to the grown-ups in the dining room. It's going better than I hoped. In the foyer, Aimee and I bid farewell to Wertheimer, who says he's off to the station to finesse some paperwork. Feeling either brave or stupid, I decide to ask him a question that's been gnawing on me since we first met.

As the detective pulls his jacket from the coat hanger, I begin: "We're almost positive that you're a Wild Card like Clyde, but if you don't mind my asking, what's your heritage combo?"

"I do mind," Wertheimer retorts, zipping up. "But you're both good eggs, and after what you've been through . . ." He hesitates at the door. "I'm a wereporcupine on my

281

mama's side, and a *Nuralagus rex sapiens* on my daddy's."
With that, he's gone.

It's not funny, except for Wertheimer's tough-guy embarrassment and the overwhelming cute factor. As I start chuckling, Aimee asks, "What's *Nura* . . . uh, *Nur* —?"

"It's a giant bunny rabbit."

Aimee and I wander onto the back porch to give Ruby and the adults privacy.

"What are you thinking about so seriously?" I ask.

"The deific. They're not such bad people . . . from a certain point of view."

I think of Luis, of all the shifters who died on the island. "Come again?"

Aimee rests her elbows on the rail. Her right hand is badly bruised, but she can bend all of her fingers. "As an intern, I was required to go to their motivational meetings. The snowmen sincerely believe that it's their destiny to use finance and technology to inherit the earth and all of its creatures, typical humans and werepeople included. Among other things, they think they'll be better custodians of the planet than we are."

That makes them sincerely lunatics, in my opinion.

"They viewed me the way most humans I know view apes," she goes on. "They considered themselves humane, letting all you shifters live in the jungle 'as nature intended' between hunts. The snowmen love. They have families

282

and family dramas. Personality conflicts and fashion faux pas. They hope for a more prosperous future. They want to live in peace. Are *Homo sapiens* so different? Are werepeople?"

I say, "For a geek, Goth, New-Age hippie girl, you're awfully deep."

We make ourselves comfortable on a couple of chaise lounges. I take it slow, mindful of my injured ribs, then pull her chair closer. "Speaking of which, you look more like yourself again."

Aimee fingers a pale-green strand in her otherwise still-white hair. "These are extensions. My colorist said that I had to wait a while before using more chemicals on it."

We stare at the stars, and she reaches to cover herself with a blanket folded on the next chair. "It's looking good for Ruby," I say. "I'm grateful to have her back." I gently bump Aimee's shoulder with mine. "To have you both home safe."

Her smile is uncertain. "You're an amazing guy, Yoshi. Good-looking, charismatic, sweeter than you think —"

"I hear a 'but' coming." I swallow hard. "That's okay. I know you have feelings for Clyde, even if he is too stupid to appreciate you." I'm referring to the Wild Card's date tonight with Noelle. Aimee looks dejected, though. I shouldn't have mentioned it.

"About that," I begin again. "About your liking him. It's not because he's a Lion, is it?" I spread my fingers around my face like a mane and put on a pouty face. "Because he has better hair than I do?"

When Aimee laughs, I hear the relief in her voice. "What *is* it with y'all werepeople and your whole food-chain, dominance-submission nonsense? I'm interested in you as individuals, as people. Also, just FYI, for humans, being attracted to animal forms is pervy and disturbed and sick."

Homo sapiens can be so narrow-minded.

Aimee swings her legs off the side of the lounge and stands. Like whatever she has to say is too important for casual chairs. "I don't want to give you a complex."

I shake my head. "You don't have to explain."

But Aimee continues: "Here's the thing. My dad bailed. My fling with Enrique fizzled." Squinting down at me, she adds, "And I've never told anyone this before, but since sixth grade, I had this crush on Jacob Feldheim, and then freshman year, he announced on Valentine's Day that he had to move to a science station in Antarctica — Antarctica — because his mother got a grant to study emperor penguins."

Penguins? Why are we talking about penguins?

"After Travis was killed, I was starting to feel cursed," she admits. "And you're . . . wow. You're not the kind of guy that a girl like me ends up with, let alone turns down. But I can't be with you just to have someone, no matter how terrific you are. I'm looking for that click, and you . . . you probably have no idea who Barbara Gordon is."

Barbara Gordon is Batgirl or Oracle, depending. A piece of trivia I picked up due to Ruby's affection for redheads. I could say so and maybe even land a second chance.

I don't. Part of being a cool Cat is knowing when to shut up.

"Clyde could be that person, if he were interested in me." Aimee's brow puckers. "In the meantime, I'm saving up to buy a hairless house cat. But I want us to stay friends, Yoshi — close friends. We may not fit that way, but we do fit. I want you in my life."

Friends. I can tell she means it.

At least I'm the first guy she ever had to let down easy. That counts for something, doesn't it? I give Aimee a brotherly hug and assure her that I understand and that I'm good with it. Or at least I will be.

After all, she's the first person besides my sister who really matters to me.

So what if my heart's breaking a little? I've gotten my family back and found the first true friend I've ever had.

YOSHI

"WHY DIDN'T YOU TELL ME?" I ask Ruby after the meeting downstairs degenerates into chocolate-hazelnut pie, coffee, and talk of football. "About the bogus internship, the interfaith coalition, your being some kind of demon-hunting secret agent?" It's not the first time I've asked. When I brought it up at the hotel and on the plane ride home, she said we'd talk later in private. When I mentioned it last night, she begged off, claiming she was still too tired. As an afterthought, I joke, "What other secrets are you keeping?"

She starts at that. "I was *sworn* to secrecy. Standard procedure, you know. I thought I was protecting you."

There's something off about Ruby's tone. It's not only that she feels guilty about almost getting us both killed, though that's part of it.

I can't quite put my finger on what's wrong. "You see how well that turned out."

We're changing the linens on a canopy bed in a second-floor bedroom at Nora's. The coalition has been keeping up with Ruby's rent, but her front door still isn't fixed, and everyone agrees that she should start over somewhere fresh.

"I called Grams," Ruby informs me. "She said something about you and a naked girl in the barn whose uncle called the sheriff on her. She mentioned gunshots, but apparently she talked her way out of it."

It's a wonder our grandmother wasn't arrested. "The girl was only *half* naked," I protest, yanking the last corner of the fitted sheet into place. "What else did Grams say?"

Ruby picks up a cornflower-blue pillowcase. "Brace yourself. She's thinking about relocating here to live with us and opening a new antiques and bonsai store."

Me and Grams, together again? I don't think so, but I'm in no mood to argue.

Ruby flicks her human-form ears. "Is it true that Noelle is with Clyde tonight?"

"Yeah," I reply, wondering why she cares. Ruby barely knows Clyde . . . but she and Noelle both had ties to Paxton. They both made the scene at Basement Blues.

Thinking back on it, the two Cat women scarcely made eye contact on the yacht or our trip home to the States.

From what I understand, Ruby turned in an Oscar-winning performance as a spy Cat. But that was performing for strangers. I know her better than anyone. She's lying.

Aimee told me about the throw-down between Noelle and Paxton back on the island, how he was her transformeaze dealer, and she . . .

Holy crap on a cracker! Paxton didn't kill Travis after all.

I can't call Clyde. Our phones were confiscated by the yetis, and neither of us has had a chance to replace them yet. But I know where they are. The Wild Card's been jabbering all day about where to take Noelle on their big date.

Bette's Barbecue is a roadside family-style restaurant nestled in the Hill Country on yet another of those Austin lakes that looks more like a river. It's a rustic place, dripping in Texana. From what I understand, it serves enormous portions of meat, which — by werepredator standards — makes it a romantic destination.

The aroma in the air is smoky delicious from the moment I step out of my car.

Once inside, I breeze past the host, saying I'm meeting friends and, continuing to the dining room, spot Clyde and Noelle at a table overlooking the murky water.

The restaurant is crowded and I can't separate out their voices in the din. However, both are scowling over platters of partially decimated ribs, sausage, and whole smoked chickens. Their sides — cole slaw, beans, and potato salad — are untouched. They've each been served a beer, suggesting that Clyde can suddenly pass for twenty-one with his fake ID, even without whiskers, and that Noelle really is about that age.

Me? I think she's too old for him and definitely too much trouble.

Both catch my scent before I reach the table, and they seem almost relieved when I sit down in an extra chair. "Hey, Clyde," I begin, reaching to rip off a chicken leg. "I need to borrow your date for a while. You don't mind, do you?"

"What're you doing here?" he asks. "I thought you were with Aimee."

He still cares about her, and part of me is too happy for them to mind.

I take my time chewing and wash it all down with a swig of Noelle's beer. Then I inform her, "This evening the cops turned Paxton over to Travis's gramps and his boys. They all think Paxton's the one who did the kid in. They're out for revenge."

I'm avoiding words like "wereperson" or "shape-shifter" or "werearmadillo" or "Cat," but Noelle understands me. She knows I know.

289

The Lion sets down her fork, her tiff with Clyde forgotten. "Why blame Paxton?" she asks. "He wasn't even —"

"Ruby told us back on Daemon Island." Clyde fiddles with his red checked napkin. "She told us that Paxton did it."

I explain, "They blamed Ruby, and knowing her, she would've sacrificed herself to save a friend, except Karl Richards — the grandfather — threatened to come after me, too, after everyone in our family, until he declared justice served."

"I had no idea." Noelle reaches into her purse. "Not about Ruby, Paxton, any of it. She probably figured he had it coming anyway, what with the drug dealing and kidnapping." Noelle tosses a handful of twenties on the table. "We were friends, Ruby and me. Just friends; I'm straight as a rail. But good friends, you know? She helped me through a rough time."

The lady Lion blows out a long breath. "Where are they, Paxton and the Dillos? Can you drive me there?"

An otherwise withdrawn Clyde insists on our taking his domino-covered SUV, which he has apparently named the Bone Chiller, to the Richards Heating & Air-Conditioning warehouse.

Noelle is silent on the drive, even when I promise to protect her.

I can't speak for Clyde, given his friendship with the

young Armadillo. He may be more of a threat to Noelle than the grieving family is. But it means something that the Lioness is coming along willingly. That she insists on trying to intervene.

Nobody protests when the speedometer hits seventy-five miles per hour in a forty-five zone.

None of us are fans of Paxton, but it would be wrong for him to die for a crime he didn't commit.

The back wheels skid as Clyde turns into the drive, and I expect him to hit the brakes. Instead, he floors the accelerator, and the Bone Chiller crashes through the metal warehouse wall.

When we jump out, Paxton is strung up, hanging by his heels, in the middle of a circle of shirtless werearmadillos, each of them holding a baseball bat. Apparently they decided to torture him first, which is awful, except that it means he's still alive.

"Stop!" Noelle shouts, running to the bleeding, battered Cat.

She extends her claws to cut him down. I rush to help while Clyde stands back, outside the circle of Dillos, taking it all in.

"What is the meaning of this?" Karl Richards demands.

As I lift Paxton onto my shoulder, Noelle says, "Address me, old man. I'm the one who killed Travis Reid. If you want to punish someone, fine. You're looking at her."

Richards tosses the bat, and it spins across the gaping

291

room, landing with a clatter on the cement floor. "No, you're trying to protect Tornquist. He's your lover."

"Not anymore," Clyde puts in. "She's telling the truth."

His Majesty's men let me haul Paxton to the SUV. He moans as I lay him out on a bench of the Bone Chiller. His jaw is shattered. He's barely conscious.

From the exertion, I've broken the scab on my side open. Now I'm bleeding, too. "Rest," I tell Paxton. "We'll get you to a healer soon."

Paxton's no innocent. There are shifters who died because he brought them to Daemon Island. But he'll have to answer separately for that to Zaleski and Wertheimer and in a way that makes us all out to be more than animals.

"I demand an explanation," Richards declares in a calmer voice, waving off his subordinates, who retreat to a small office toward the rear of the warehouse.

Noelle stays where she is, holding the hangman's rope like it belongs to her.

I casually position myself between the lady Lion and Richards, glancing from one to the other. "You followed Ruby that night," I say to Noelle. "You followed her and Travis into the park. You and my sister were friends, but something was wrong."

Noelle nods. "We weren't getting along. She didn't understand why I kept crawling back to Paxton. Ruby insisted I could succeed as a singer in fully human form — not only on the shifter circuit but anywhere.

"I was worried about her, too. I thought she was keeping secrets. I didn't understand the change in her, the provocative way she suddenly dressed and acted. She smelled as if she was afraid for her life."

"Davidson Morris was a vampire," Clyde explains. "Ruby got close enough to find out what he and his buddies were up to, and then she staked him to hell. It was one of those covert, heroic, save-the-world things. Ruby is one of the good guys."

"Oh," Richards and Noelle breathe.

It's satisfying, hearing the Wild Card sing my sister's praises.

"The night Travis died, you were using transformeaze," Clyde says. "Weren't you, Noelle? Do you even remember what happened?" His tone is more sad than angry. "Do you even remember killing my oldest and best friend?"

Tears trickle down Noelle's cheeks, but she keeps her head up. "The first thing I remember is Ruby tearing me off his already dead body. She tried to stop me. I don't know what happened exactly. I must've lost all semblance of control, doubled back in Lion form, and by the time she —"

"It was too late." His Majesty draws his revolver. "I lost my beloved grandson because of your ambition, your weakness, your predatory nature, because you're a Cat."

Clyde grabs his arm. "Enough killing! Noelle needs help. She didn't mean to —"

"This isn't a court of law," Richards thunders. "I don't

care about intent. My grandbaby, my sweet young prince, suffered a horrible, painful, bloody death because of that woman. Why shouldn't I have justice? Why shouldn't I take a life for a life?"

"Because, Pop-Pop, I'm asking you not to," replies a disembodied voice.

Goose bumps rise on my skin, but Clyde doesn't look surprised. There's more to him than I first realized, and not just because of his Lion within.

Meanwhile, Richards gapes at his grandson's spirit, hovering protectively over Noelle. "Oh, Travis," he whispers, lowering the gun.

CLYDE

AFTER LEAVING THE OTHERS in Nora's care, I text Aimee on my way home from the warehouse and ask her to meet me at Travis's shrine at the chain-link fence in the neighborhood park. In addition to saving Noelle's life, he was right about my feelings for Aimee. I only hope that she can see past Yoshi to give me a chance.

Seated on the walk with her gypsy-style skirt tucked around her legs, Aimee has beaten me there by long enough to light a few blue votive candles.

"Any word from Quincie, Kieren, and Zachary?" I ask.

Aimee does that cute crinkling thing with her forehead.

"No, but Nora did say something to the effect that they were having a hell of a time in New England, whatever that's supposed to mean. I think they may have run into car trouble or something."

They'll show up soon enough. School starts again on Monday.

"I'm getting rid of my SUV," I say. "The Bone Chiller has done what I hoped, saved a shifter from other shifters. It wasn't as much fun as I thought it'd be."

"You saved someone *with the car*?" Aimee asks, knowing it was parked here in Austin while we were on the island. "Who was your sidekick on this mission?"

"Yoshi," I reply, though it was more of a team effort.

"*Yoshi* was your sidekick," she muses. "So you don't still hate him?"

"Unfortunately not." Which isn't to say I'm crazy about the guy, either.

With her good hand, she tugs me down to sit with her. "How mature of you both."

On a roll, I add, "I've decided to donate my wheels to the interfaith coalition so that the domino bones of those shifters fight on with good guys."

"Very poetic." Aimee reaches to cuddle a stuffed toy armadillo. "Have you talked to your parents yet?"

About the whole paternity, bi-species issue, she means. "Not yet, but I will. My mom first, and then we should probably talk to my dad together. Meanwhile, I'm still a

Possum, too. Now when I shift, I can pick between my Possum or Lion forms."

"Your dad loves you," Aimee says, as usual cutting through the crap to the heart of the issue. "And whatever was going on with your folks back then, they're long over it. They've moved on together." When I don't reply, she adds, "How's Noelle?"

The Lioness will survive, thanks to the bond between Travis and his grandfather. I had such a strong reaction when I met her, and, in different ways, Yoshi and even Ruby before that. Having spent my whole life in a Possum family, it may have taken getting to know Noelle to call forth my Lion heritage.

"She's probably still pissed at me," I say. "We broke up . . . not that we'd really gotten *together* together, but anyway, she has more serious things to worry about now. My backing off, it just hurt her pride." I'm overexplaining. "Get it? Lion? Pride?"

I sound like a goof, and not in a good way. "Don't mind me," I say. "I might as well be playing dead." Again. "Want to bring me back to life with a kiss?"

Her laugh is tentative. "I'm not a fairy-tale girl."

Aimee's always been the courageous one. She kisses me anyway. Her lips are soft and tentative, her teeth demure, and her tongue tinged with tomato sauce. It's not all passion and heat like Noelle, but it's more real somehow, more satisfying.

With Aimee, I can do more than battle evildoers. I can watch sci-fi and play D&D and maybe even hit the paint-ball range someday.

Travis was right. Nobody fits with me, the whole me, better than she does. Aimee is the Barbara Gordon/ Batgirl/Oracle to my Dick Grayson/Robin/Nightwing.

No, the Dinah Lance/Black Canary to my Oliver Queen/Green Arrow!

How I dig a hot blonde in fishnets!

All we need now is tights and capes.

AUTHOR'S NOTE

Feral Nights is set in a fantastical multi-creature-verse that serves as a stage for many of my novels, and the events in *Feral Nights* are simultaneous to those in *Diabolical*, my immediately preceding book.

Diabolical, along with *Tantalize*, *Eternal*, and *Blessed*, was inspired by Bram Stoker's classic, *Dracula*. Those four books may be read either as stand-alone novels or together to form what we authors call a super-arc. Big, building story. Big payoff.

You get the idea.

Feral Nights isn't part of that conversation with Stoker or its overarching story line. It's a spin-off, a new story line, but one with roots. Some of the settings, characters, and plot threads were introduced in the earlier quartet.

Feral Nights grew out of letters from readers asking for more of popular secondary characters like Clyde, Aimee, and Brenek. It grew out of questions like "What ever happened to Ruby Kitahara?" and "Where did that werebear rug come from?"

Around the same time, I became ever more fascinated with the question of whether, over the ages, different species of the *Homo* genus have shared the earth at the same time.

I'd already begun to explore that idea by including the various species of natural-born shifters alongside *Homo sapiens* in the fantasy universe, when it occurred to me to wonder, What if there was another branch of the family tree — an older yet crafty and sophisticated one — prospering unknown to the rest of the world?

That said, *Feral Nights* is written especially for everyone who's told me — if not in so many words — that they loved spooky adventure and sweeping romance and inspiring gallantry but saw themselves more as a first mate, a second-stringer, or a best *amigo*.

Speaking of y'all readers . . . Although the *character* of Cameron isn't based on him, a student named Cameron that I met during a Houston/Pasadena area high school visit suggested I use his name in my next novel, preferably in connection to a demon king. Consider it done.

On a related note, the fictional Cameron's mention of "hobbits" was a reference to *Homo floresiensis*, not the works of J. R. R. Tolkien. Just in case you were worried.

Avid readers and pop-culture fans may also notice references to Aesop, L. Frank Baum, Pierre Boulle, Johnny Capps,

Lewis Carroll, Chris Carter, Bob Clampett, Richard Connell, Clarissa Pinkola Estés, Bill Finger, Ian Fleming, Gardner Fox, Gary Friedrich, William Golding, Hanna-Barbera, John Hughes, Carmine Infantino, Michael Jackson, Julian Jones, Bob Kane, Robert Kanigher, Rudyard Kipling, Jack Kirby, Noel Langley, Glen A. Larson, Stan Lee, C. S. Lewis, George Lucas, Bela Lugosi, Robert McKimson, Irene Mecchi, Jake Michie, General Mills, Sheldon Moldoff, Julian Murphy, Andrew Nance, George Papp, Charles Perrault, Mike Ploog, Jonathan Roberts, Jerry Robinson, Gene Roddenberry, Joe Ruby, Florence Ryerson, Louis Sachar, Franklin J. Schaffner, Leon Schlesinger Productions, Joe Shuster, Jerry Siegel, Ken Spears, Sir Henry Morton Stanley, David Stern, Jimmy Stewart, Roy Thomas, John Updike, Manuel R. Vega, John Walsh, Mort Weisinger, H. G. Wells, Joss Whedon, E. B. White, Woodrow Wilson, Edgar Allan Woof, Linda Woolverton, and Brian Yansky (who would make a fine necromancer, if he ever set his mind to it).

Alas, Daemon Island, Enlightenment Alley, Basement Blues, and Sanguini's are fictional locales, as are the characters' homes and various referenced publications. My apologies if you're disappointed. I'd dearly love to sample Nora's cognac-cream fettuccine Alfredo with broiled alligator and pine nuts, too.

On a final note, when Clyde and Aimee muse on themselves as a parallel couple to Dick and Barbara or Ollie and Dinah, they're thinking of the good times.

As Aimee says, "Love is scary hard, even for superheroes."

It's also worth it.

ACKNOWLEDGMENTS

My deepest appreciation to my editor, Deborah Noyes; her assistant, Carter Hasegawa; my paperback editor, Hilary Van Dusen; and the additional editorial/production/design/ marketing/sales rock stars — especially Tracy and Jenny — who, day after day, make magic in the form of books.

I'd also like to thank my agent, Ginger Knowlton; her assistant, Anna Umansky; and the whole team at Curtis Brown Ltd.

Closer to home, cheers to the Austin children's and YA literature community, particularly P. J. Hoover and Lisa Parker; to my very cute husband, Greg Leitich Smith; and to our own merry band of (were?)cats — Mercury, Bashi, Blizzard, and Leo, who raise the expression "wild things" to a whole new level.

CYNTHIA LEITICH SMITH is the acclaimed and best-selling author of *Tantalize*, *Eternal*, *Blessed*, and *Diabolical*, as well as *Tantalize: Kieren's Story*, and *Eternal: Zachary's Story*, two graphic novels illustrated by Ming Doyle. About *Feral Nights*, she says, "The world is vast and mysterious, but it may well be that its biggest secrets are the ones lurking — unknown even to us — within ourselves." Cynthia lives in Austin, Texas, with her husband, author Greg Leitich Smith.